A Company
of Fools

Published in Canada by Fitzhenry & Whiteside,
195 Allstate Parkway, Markham, Ontario L3R 4T8

Published in the United States by Fitzhenry & Whiteside,
311 Washington Street, Brighton, Massachusetts 02135

www.fitzhenry.ca   godwit@fitzhenry.ca

10 9 8 7 6 5 4 3

Library and Archives Canada Cataloguing in Publication
Ellis, Deborah, 1960-
A company of fools / Deborah Ellis.
ISBN 978-1-55455-072-2
1. Black Death--France--Juvenile fiction. I. Title.
PS8559.L5494C65 2008   jC813'.54   C2007-906142-7

U.S. Publisher Cataloging-in-Publication Data
(Library of Congress Standards)
Ellis, Deborah, 1960-
The company of fools / Deborah Ellis.
Originally published: 2002.
[192] p. : cm.
Summary: Henri has been living within abbey walls all his life, first
in the care of nuns, then as a choirboy and scribe. When Micah arrives, his
voice and presence bring a fresh breeze into dead places. Together,
both must learn to live through difficult times.
ISBN 978-1-1554-55072-2 (pbk.)
1. Monks — Juvenile fiction. 2. Choirboys — Juvenile fiction. 3. Black Death
–France — Juvenile fiction. I. Title.
[Fic] dc22   PZ7.E469Co 2007

Fitzhenry & Whiteside acknowledges with thanks the Canada Council
for the Arts, and the Ontario Arts Council for their support of our publishing
program. We acknowledge the financial support of the Government of Canada
through the Book Publishing Industry Development Program (BPIDP)
for our publishing activities.

 **Canada Council
for the Arts** **Conseil des Arts
du Canada**

Interior design by Wycliffe Smith Design Inc.
Cover design by Sandra Nobes
Cover illustration by Larry Brownstein / Getty Images
Author's photo by John Spray
Edited by Laura Peetoom
Plague map (page 187) by Paul Heersink
Thanks to Dr. Ian Storey
Printed in Canada

A Company of Fools

Fitzhenry & Whiteside

TO MY MOTHER, FATHER, AND SISTER

— Đ.Æ.

PROLOGUE

✦✝✦

I, HENRI, CHOIR STUDENT AT THE ABBEY OF ST. LUC, near Paris, do now in the Year of Our Lord 1349 set down for the sake of history the wondrous and sorrowful events which took place in the time of Pestilence, that those who follow might come to know that there was such a time of trouble, and such a boy as Micah.

I have in mind a sort of chronicle. Of course, a real chronicler writes down events as they happen. I did not do that—I was too busy being alive. But the events I want to chronicle occurred not so long ago. They are still fresh and vivid in my mind, so vivid that my memories rob me of sleep. I seek the comfort of pen on parchment, to clear my head of all that disturbs me.

I will begin with the day Micah came to the abbey.

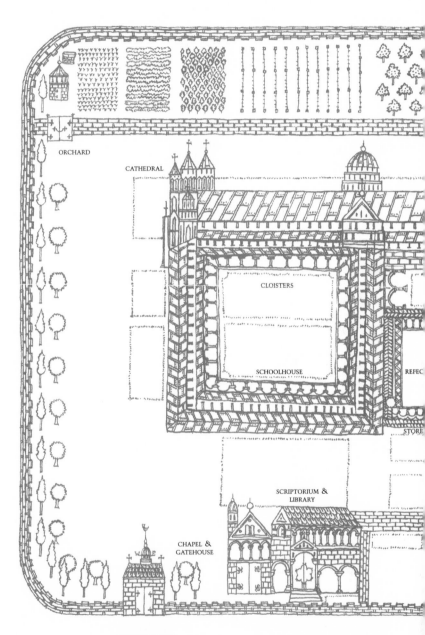

ORCHARD

CATHEDRAL

CLOISTERS

SCHOOLHOUSE

REFEC

STORE

SCRIPTORIUM &
LIBRARY

CHAPEL &
GATEHOUSE

ABBEY ENTRANCE

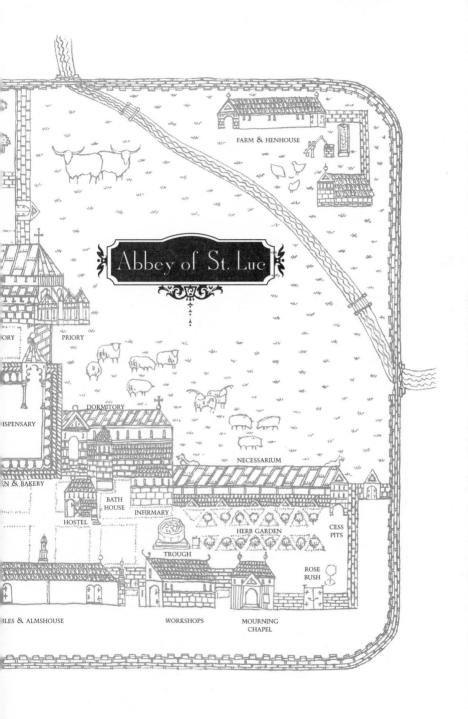

CHAPTER ONE

❖✝❖

"I see a flock of giant crows," Fabien announced.

He was looking out the window of the choirboys' vestry, daydreaming as usual instead of hanging up his surplice.

I was close enough to the window to see the monks spilling out of the cathedral and running across the green. Their black habits flapped behind them like wings.

My view was quickly blocked by Gaston. "What are they up to?" he wondered. "Come here, the rest of you—look at this."

The other eight choirboys gathered at the window, pushing and shoving so they could see. Arlo and I kept to our business; Arlo, because he was head boy and generally beyond shoving; me, because I'd never shoved another boy in my life.

"Brother Bart must be back," one of the boys yelled. They all bolted for the door.

"Take off your surplices," Arlo ordered.

White vestments fluttered in the air, most landing

on hooks, as the boys obeyed Arlo before running outside. Arlo looked at the mess on the floor, then at the tempting open door, and ran out to join the excitement.

I shrugged myself out of my surplice, hung it properly on the hook, and hung up the surplices that had landed on the floor. It was in no one's best interest to make Brother James angry. He was in charge of the vestments.

That done, I began to feel foolish, all by myself in the vestry, and headed out after the other choirboys. They were easy to spot, their cassocks red against the green of the new spring grass.

I caught up with them at the gatehouse. Once again, they were pushing each other to see in the window, a task made harder by the window being higher than any of them was tall.

"Oswin, get down on your knees and let Gaston stand on your back," Arlo directed in a quiet voice. Standing at the gatehouse window spying on the monks wasn't strictly forbidden in Saint Benedict's Rule, which ran our lives, but it wasn't expressly allowed, either.

Gaston, on his perch, sent whispered reports back to the rest of us.

"It *is* Brother Bart," he said.

"What did he bring back with him?"

"I can't see that, but the Prior looks angry."

"The Prior always looks angry," Joris pointed out. "What about Father Abbot? If he's angry, then Brother Bart is really in trouble."

Although this last sentence was uttered with some glee, it was not out of a wish to see Brother Bart in trouble again. We were all fond of him, but choir school is a dull place. Even the least adventurous of us, which I confess is myself, likes a bit of drama now and then.

"The Prior is angry, the Abbot looks confused, and Brother Bart looks excited," Gaston reported.

"Why are we standing here?" Rafe, the youngest choirboy, asked me. He hadn't been at the abbey for very long.

"You know Brother Bart?"

"The big one? Of course. He's fun."

"He plays with us," Reverdy chirped in. He was next-to-youngest, and Rafe's best friend.

"He's been away, and every time he goes away he brings something back. We're waiting here to see what he's brought back this time."

"I thought monks were supposed to stay behind the walls," Rafe said, pointing to the high stone walls that went all the way around the abbey grounds.

"They are, but Brother Bart has wandering feet. Every now and then his feet take him out of the abbey. The Abbot lets him. Wandering feet is a theological condition," I added, unsure of my ground, but wanting to impress the young ones.

"And he always brings something back?" Reverdy asked.

"Foolish things," Bayard said. "A scrawny chicken, a miserable cat, a muddy stick, things like that."

"The chicken is the best egg-layer in the abbey henhouse," Arlo said, "and the muddy stick turned into a rosebush."

"But the cat is still miserable," Bayard insisted.

I said nothing, even though I knew more about the cat than the others.

Gaston made waving motions with his hands to shut us up. "There are too many monks in the way. They're looking down at something, and shaking their heads, but I can't see what they're frowning at." Perhaps sensing that his report wasn't interesting, he added to it. "Wait—the Prior is turning green. He's taken off his shoe and is hitting Brother Bart on the head with it."

"That's enough." Arlo yanked him down from Oswin's back, and pulled me forward. "Up you go," he said to me. "We need someone up there we can depend on."

I clung to the window ledge and peered inside. All I could see was monks, but I could hear Brother Bart.

"Father Abbot, I had to bring him here. They were going to hang him!"

"A criminal!" That was the Prior's voice.

"But still a child," said Father Abbot, calmly. "Now that you've brought him here, Brother Bartholemew, what do you propose to do with him?"

All the monks whose faces I could see were looking down and frowning. Then the wall of black robes parted, and I saw what they were frowning at.

I got my first look at Micah.

His clothes were more rags than garments, and he was all-over filthy. Straw stuck out of his matted hair, and there was so much dirt on his face, it was hard for me to tell what he looked like. He was small, like me, but not sickly. He looked like he could handle himself in a fight.

Another rough boy, I thought with disappointment. We already had plenty of those.

"It's just a boy," I said without interest, stepping down from Oswin's back. "Brother Bart brought back a boy."

Gaston quickly took my place. I went to the edge of the group, and was about to make a solitary walk back to the schoolhouse when a sound reached my ears. It was the sound of singing.

I'd arrived at St. Luc's when I was five, and before that, I'd spent four years with the nuns. I'd spent all my life around choirs and music, and the sound of yet another boy raising his voice in song should have done nothing to me. But so moved was I that I did something no one would ever have imagined me doing.

I shoved Gaston out of the way, and re-took my place on Oswin's back. Gaston was too shocked to object, but I would not have heard him anyway.

Micah, covered in grime and stink, hands defiantly on his hips, was singing about a drunken bishop who cracked his head open on the cathedral steps and the crows feasted on his brain. The song was foolish and profane, shocking most of the monks, although I saw a smile play on the mouths of Brother Bart and Brother Marc. But the voice singing it was...unearthly.

"What is your name, lad?" Father Abbot asked when the song was over.

"My name is Micah," he replied, not at all humble in front of the great holy man.

"Micah was one of the holy prophets," said Father Abbot. "Who knows? Under all that filth, you may share some of his qualities." He turned to Brother Bart. "Clean him up. We'll see if we can make a choirboy out of him." He started out of the gatehouse.

"Hey!"

This yell came from Micah. I was so shocked that anyone would talk that way to the Abbot, I almost fell off Oswin's back.

The Abbot looked at Micah. "Is there something you wish to add?"

"I haven't said whether I feel like staying or not."

The Abbot waited. "Well?"

Micah gave the matter a moment's thought, then shrugged his shoulders and said, "I guess I'll try it for a while."

"Heaven be praised," the Abbot said, rolling his eyes. "Brother Bartholemew, he is your responsibility."

That final statement was too much for the Prior, and he started sputtering. "But Brother Bart fails at everything!"

"Calm yourself, Father Prior," the Abbot said. "How much trouble can one small boy be?"

I studied Micah, and wondered.

Brother Bart brought Micah out of the gate-house. The other boys got their first look at him.

"He doesn't look like much," Gaston said.

"I'm worth an army of any of you," retorted Micah, his hands curling into fists. His clothes were rags, and there was a strange thing on his back. When he turned around, I saw it had a long neck, a round bottom, and strings running its length.

Brother Bart put a hand on Micah's shoulder. "We're off to the washhouse," he said. "Henri, come with us. You and Micah will likely be partners in procession, so you might as well get to know each other."

I was not sure I liked that idea. The end spot had always been mine, ever since I was seven and just a probationer in the choir. The monks could see even then that I had the temperament for it. All other boys as they came were fitted into pairs, but I was left on my own.

"That's right, Henri. You take care of the new boy," Arlo said, comfortably handing responsibility for Micah over to me. My displeasure must have shown on my face, because Micah said, "Me, partner with that? He's so pale, he's little more than a ghost. Anyway, I sing alone."

"He'll take some beating into shape," observed Fabien cheerfully.

"Wait until he meets Brother Beltran's palmer," Bayard added, referring to the long stick Brother Beltran hit us with when we misbehaved. Hit them, I mean, as I never misbehaved.

Brother Bart, in that mild, steady way of his, drew me to him and marched us both off to the washhouse.

Brother Gulian, in charge there, blocked our way in at the door. "I'm not having such a filthy creature getting into one of my clean washtubs."

"Charity, good Brother," pleaded Brother Bart.

"For charity, go to the almshouse. I'll have the cobbler and the clothing monk meet you there."

St. Luc's, being a prosperous abbey, has, in addition to a hostel for merchant travelers, a large almshouse, where the poor can get a bowl of pottage and some straw to sleep on. There is a trough there for the watering of horses, and this is where Brother Gulian intended Brother Bart should give Micah a bath.

"In you go, lad," Brother Bart said, nodding at the trough.

"What for?" Micah asked.

"To get clean."

"What for?"

Brother Bart had no answer. Nor did I. The monks practiced strict rules of cleanliness, bathing four times a year. The choirboys did likewise. No one had ever asked why.

"Off with those clothes and into the water," Brother Bart said.

"You want me to do what?" Micah hugged his rags close to him. "You're not stealing my clothes!"

Brother Peter, in charge of the almshouse, was a small monk, gentle and kind. I had assisted him there from time to time, and had seen him comfort many an agitated soul. Micah was more than he could handle. But then Brother Nestor, the cobbler, arms strong from the cutting and shaping of leather, came into the almshouse yard carrying several sizes of wooden clog sandals. With him was Brother Algernon, who squinted from so many hours bent over his sewing table. He took care of our ordinary clothes.

Micah glared at them while they held a whispered consultation with Brother Bart. The group broke apart, and quickly, Brother Bart took the object off Micah's back and handed it to me. Then the four monks picked Micah up and plopped him in the trough.

Such a string of yells and curses! I am sure the abbey walls never heard before nor will ever hear again the sound of fury that came from Brother Bart's latest find. I was amazed that the same boy who could create a noise that was painfully beautiful could also create a noise that was just painful.

It occurred to me suddenly that Micah had never had a bath before.

I pondered this notion a while, until Micah's screeching ceased to be amusing and became offensive. I turned away, intending to go into the almshouse to see if I could be of assistance within. I was stopped by the sight of a man leaning against the wall.

Out of long habit, I checked this new face, to see if it looked like mine, in case my father had somehow made his way to me from the bottom of the sea. But all I saw in the face was weariness.

"You can go inside," I told him. "You will be made welcome."

"I am so tired," the man said.

"There is clean straw to sleep on," I said, taking his arm to guide him to the door.

"I no longer sleep, boy." The man's voice was low, more an animal growl than human speech. I don't know how I heard it through Micah's screeching. It frightened me, and I withdrew my hand from his arm and backed away.

"I cannot close my eyes to sleep, when the end of time is coming. I must tell everyone, boy. I must tell you."

I backed up, but he came after me, until I was pressed into a corner with no escape. His eyes were on fire, and his face came from a nightmare.

"I was the harbormaster in Marseille," he began.

I do not remember now the exact words of his terrible tale, and for that I am grateful. Even though I was soon to see all the horrors of the Plague for myself, it is the harbormaster's tale that haunts my darkest nights.

A ship drifted into his harbor, its sails drooping. There were no greetings rising up from the deck, no faces of sailors, weary of each other's company. Only silence. The harbormaster, fearing scurvy or a mutiny, sent out a skiff full of men to investigate. When they jumped, screaming, into the sea, he went out himself.

"Death was on that ship!" he spat out. "Death with a face more horrible than it has ever shown before, black, bloody, and putrid."

He walked among the bodies, to see if there was anyone left alive, but all were dead, from the captain on down to the prisoners in the brig.

I saw the man wilt a little then, as if the memory of what he had seen was too heavy to bear, and my heart flashed for him a moment of pity. The harbormaster then told me how, when he returned to shore and ordered the ship towed out to sea and burned, his order was disobeyed and the ship's hold looted of its cargo.

"The people of Marseille paid for their greed," he said. "Death got off the ship and rowed into the harbor, perhaps hidden in a bolt of cloth, perhaps disguised as a vat of olives. It grabbed hold of the people by the throat, turning them mad, turning them against each other. It was a race to see whom Death could kill first, the rats or the citizens. Both ended up in piles on the streets.

"I knew then that I had to leave my city. I left my wife and children for Death to devour. I spend my days and nights walking and telling those I meet what I have seen."

The man rose up again. He grabbed hold of me and pulled me close to him, so that our noses were together, and my feet dangled in the air. His breath was foul as he howled into my face, "Death is coming, Boy! The end of the world! Prepare yourself! Memento mori! Memento mori!"

The screams that filled the almshouse then came from me. In the next instant, I was on the floor, and the twisted man was rubbing his head and being hustled away by Brother Peter into the almshouse.

Brother Bart picked up the sandal that had bounced off the harbormaster's head, and returned it to Micah. "Good aim," he said to Micah, as he helped me to my feet.

Micah, now dressed in the gray tunic and jerkin we choirboys wear when not at services, grabbed his property out of my hand.

"You'd better not have broken it," he said.

I didn't know whether to be grateful or annoyed. I decided to be both.

CHAPTER THREE

◆✠◆

I had never seen anyone so small eat so much.

We were eating in the monks' refectory, where choirboys dined only on rare feast days. The long wooden benches and tables were empty, except for us. Micah downed his portions of stew and bread in almost one gulp. When Brother Bart passed his own over, he ate that, too.

I have never been a heavy eater. My appetite was further cooled on this day by sitting across from this strange boy. Micah eyed the remainders of my dinner. I remembered how he threw his shoe at the crazy man, and I pushed the rest of my meal over the table to him.

"Tell me about this," Brother Bart asked Micah, touching the object he'd had strapped to his back, which was now on the table beside him.

Micah's mouth was full, so I took the opportunity to ask, "What is it?"

"It's a lute," Brother Bart told me, his fingers gently stroking the strings. I liked the sound they made as his fingers drew across them. "It's not used in the cathedral, so I'm not surprised you've never seen one."

"It was my father's," Micah said, swallowing what was in his mouth. "He was a troubador. He's dead."

"How?" asked Brother Bart.

"Fever," he replied, matter-of-factly. "He died when my mother died. The fever took both of them."

"When was this?" Brother Bart asked; then, at Micah's blank stare, "How many winters ago?"

There is no point in asking how many to someone who can't count.

"I was smaller," Micah said. "Now I'm bigger." He shoved the last bit of bread in his mouth and looked around, perhaps for something more to eat.

"Let me tell you a bit about what your life here will be like," Brother Bart said to Micah. "It will be very different from your life in Paris."

Micah pulled at the collar of his tunic. I was sure it itched him. He would soon get used to it.

"Everyone has a job here," Brother Bart continued. "Brother Marc, for example, is our chief illuminator, and draws pictures in the books in the scriptorium. Brother Kenneth is in charge of the wine cellar. My job is to clean out the cesspits. Your job will be to go to school and sing in the choir. Brother Paul, the choirmaster, will teach you how to sing."

"I know how to sing."

"You know how to sing for the people of Paris. Singing in a cathedral is different."

Micah shrugged. "Singing is singing. I open my mouth, people smile."

"In the cathedral, you'll be singing to please God, not people," I said, then wanted to bite my tongue off. I sounded like the Prior.

"If God wants to give me money for singing, that would be fine with me," Micah said. "So far, he's been pretty stingy."

I did not know what to think of this talk. Brother Bart did not seem ruffled by it. But then, he had been a soldier before he joined the Benedictines, and must have heard much blaspheming.

I turned away, so as to not have to decide how to react. Micah kept talking with Brother Bart for a while; their voices made a pleasing echo around the stone walls.

"Please wait here while I see if the physician is free," Brother Bart said at last. "I will return in a moment."

He left me alone with Micah, but I did not turn around. I kept my thoughts and sights on the refectory. I was trying to imagine what the hall was like when the monks were at their meal, silently signing to the servers for water, salt, or vinegar. The lector, in his pulpit high on the wall, would be reading from the sacred texts so the monks' minds would be on lofty matters while they took care of the baser needs of their bodies. This was where I would take all my meals for the rest of my life, once I changed my choirboy cassock for a monk's cowl and habit. I would be one of the black robes bent over the table. I would take my turn reading from the pulpit and washing the stone floor, as so many have done before. This is the way it would be, soon and always.

Bang, bang, bang—the noise drove my thoughts away. I turned from my contemplation of the refectory to see Micah banging on the three upturned wooden bowls with his mug. He went from one to the other, faster then slower, in a rhythm that I'd never heard in the abbey before.

He began singing to himself, a foolish tune, without real words. I heard his feet shuffle on the stone floor, saw him frown. Then, to my great horror, I saw him climb up onto the bench then onto the table. He tapped his feet on the thick wood surface and smiled at the sound, as it bounced against the stone walls. Then the whole refectory echoed with the clatter of wood on wood to the tune of wordless singing.

I was too stunned to move or speak. It didn't matter. Micah wasn't dancing for me. He was dancing for himself. I know that now. He was dancing because his belly was full, he was warm and dry, and he was still alive when he should have been hanged. If I had been him, I would have danced on the table, too.

But at that time, I was terrified that God would strike him down, and me with him, for watching. Fortunately, Brother Bart returned before God found the source of the profane noise. Brother Bart took Micah's hand and helped him down from the table-top, even though I'm certain Micah could have leapt down himself.

"Brother Sebastien is able to see you now," he said to Micah. "Henri, will you take him over to the infirmary, and then give him a tour of our abbey? I must clean out my cesspits."

"I have some Latin to study," I mumbled. I hated saying no to Brother Bart, but I felt shy at being alone with this strange boy. If he would dance on the top of a refectory table, what other strange things would he do?

"The pits can wait a little longer, then," Brother Bart said, cheerfully.

"What's Latin?" Micah asked.

"You heard Latin this morning," Brother Bart replied before I could express my shock at someone not knowing something so basic. "The man in the almshouse shouted 'Memento mori.' That's the Latin language."

"Memento mori," Micah repeated. "What does it mean?"

"Henri, you have a fine mind for Latin. You tell us."

"Memento mori." I thought quickly. Having just

been complimented on my ability, it wouldn't do to get this wrong. "Remember death?" I ventured.

"That is exactly right. He was shouting, 'Remember death.'"

"Paris is full of people hollering things," Micah said. We started walking out of the refectory.

"Do you know what the message was, Henri?" Brother Bart asked me.

"He was saying that Death is coming, and we should be thinking about it. *Is* Death coming?" Fear ran through me again. "Is it true, what he said?"

"Death is always coming," Brother Bart said. "To some people, 'Memento mori' is a motto, the way they lead their lives. But I don't like it as a motto. I have seen much of Death, and I do not like to think about it. It will come when it comes. I prefer 'Dum vivimus, vivamus.'"

I was glad he didn't ask me to translate that phrase as well.

"'While we live, let us live,'" he said. "Let us be joyful to be alive, and happy at all the good things around us."

We emerged from the refectory into the bright spring day.

"How can we think of Death on such a beautiful day?" Brother Bart asked us. "Let us laugh and be brave. If Death comes, he'll see people who are cheerful and not afraid, and perhaps he'll think we're not worth the trouble. Laugh with me, boys."

Brother Bart began laughing, at nothing at all. His big, jolly laugh swelled out over the abbey grounds.

It took no prodding to get Micah to laugh, but I was still not used to it. Still, I did not want to be left out, so I did my best.

Our laughter set the ducks to quacking. The chickens in the henhouse started squawking, and the birds in the orchard began chirping.

We laughed until we were breathless, until the joy of our noise pushed the stranger's tale of death out of our minds.

Brother Bart put his arm around Micah's shoulder, and they headed off to the infirmary.

I turned in the direction of the schoolhouse, but as I heard them laughing across the green, I wished I was going with them.

CHAPTER FOUR

I am writing this in a vacant study carrel in the scriptorium. It used to belong to Brother Probus, who was taken from us by the Plague.

There are many other empty desks. I like this one, because it is close to the fireplace. It is December now, and even though there is a brazier of coals hanging from the desk to help warm my fingers, the stone walls and floors cling to the cold as if it were a comfort to them.

Micah became such a large part of my life that the time before he came to St. Luc's seems as vacant and dry as a Bible desert. As I look back now on his early days here, I am reminded of a fresh, cool breeze that sweeps through a musty crypt, taking away the dead air and filling it with stuff that's sweet to breathe and good for the lungs. But only a windstorm has strength enough to blow freshness through dead places. That was Micah.

I smile, as I write this. I think he would enjoy being likened to a windstorm.

By the time I came to St. Luc's, four years of living with the nuns had prepared me for monastery life. The other boys, too, came here already schooled in the manners and traditions of the Benedictines. They had attended parish song schools, or had private tutors. They knew some Latin, and they knew how to sit still.

Micah knew none of those things.

He knew how to beg, how to steal, and how to run from a beating. He knew how to find warmth in a cold city, and a companion on a lonely night.

He did not know how to comb his hair, walk in line when he felt like running, wait his turn, or follow anyone's whim but his own.

He was a stranger in a strange land.

If it had been me, I would have found a way to disappear inside myself until the strangeness wore off, and everyone stopped taking notice of me. Micah was not like me. It was not in his nature to disappear. It was in his nature to fight. When the other choirboys taunted him over his rough manners, or his tall tales, or his ignorance, he would reply with his fists, a windstorm, stirring things up and making a mess.

"Henri, take care of him," Brother Bart said, as he dropped Micah off at the schoolhouse that evening on his way to join the other monks at prayer.

Micah ignored me, walking right past me into

the center of the room. His lute was slung across his tunic. He circled the room, looking each of the choirboys in the eye.

"You've never seen anyone like me before," he said.

"We've seen lots of boys," Arlo said. "What makes you so different?"

"I was almost hanged," Micah replied. "Can any of you make that claim?"

We could not.

"I suppose you're going to tell us all about it," Arlo said. He was not impressed by bragging. He was impressed by a fine point of logic, or a beautiful angle in geometry. He planned to go to the university in Paris when he was old enough.

"It's too bad you all missed it," Micah said with a swagger. "You probably don't get much excitement in this place. It happened just outside the prison. A huge crowd came to see me hang, because I'm the worst criminal in all of Paris. They were all yelling for me to die, but I laughed in their faces. I waited until the hangman came close enough to put the rope around my neck. Then I kicked him so hard he fell off the scaffold. I jumped into the crowd and got away. Father Abbot begged me to come here, because in addition to being the biggest criminal, I'm also the best singer in Paris."

"Well, you're the biggest braggart, anyway," Arlo said. "Henri, you'll have your work cut out for you."

"Oh, is he *your* friend, Henri?" Oswin asked. "We needn't bother with him, then."

"What's this thing around your neck?" Gaston reached for the lute, and Micah was engaged in the first of many fistfights.

Arlo separated them, and Micah launched into another tale of his bravery on the streets of Paris. I had heard enough. I climbed the stairs to the dormitory.

I crawled under my cot and brought up a parcel, wrapped in a cloth. I sat on my bed, and unwrapped my father's astrolabe.

My mother died giving birth to me. My father was a sea captain, and he gave me to the nuns to care for, temporarily, while he went to sea. A year later, his first mate returned, saying my father was dead, leaving me his astrolabe.

Micah was sure his father was dead.

I was sure my father was alive.

I believed, then, that he had been swallowed by a whale, like Jonah. He had a room, deep in the whale's belly, with a bed and a sea chest. There was a cook-fire there, where he cooked the fish that swam down the whale's throat. He was waiting for his astrolabe so he could find his way home.

And still, after everything, I plan one day to go to the ocean and throw the astrolabe in the water, so that it might be found and swallowed by that whale, and land safe in my father's hands.

I stood at the dormitory window that evening, hugging the astrolabe, as Micah's bragging voice rose and fell with each tale he told. I thought about the harbormaster's story, and I missed the father I never knew.

The next few days were just as stormy for Micah as the first.

At mealtimes he pushed to get to the food first, then took more than his share and refused to give any back. In Latin class, he balanced his hornbook on his head, and wandered around the schoolhouse, sometimes dancing, sometimes just pacing.

"He's just another of Brother Bart's disasters," Hugh said to Antoine. Normally, that sort of comment during Latin class would have resulted in a whack from Brother Beltran's palmer, but Brother Beltran evidently shared Hugh's opinion, and did not punish him.

I could not concentrate on my studies. My eyes kept turning to Micah. There was something about him that made me want to watch him, and it was more than the tapping of his feet in time to our recitation of Latin verbs. I wonder now if it was because he seemed, like me, to be alone.

"When do I get to sing?" he demanded, interrupting the class.

Brother Beltran pointed to the door and said, "Now. Henri, take him over to the cathedral. Perhaps Brother Paul can do something with him."

I was shy as we crossed the green. I did not know what to say to this strange boy. I thought about pointing out some of the features of the abbey—the stables, perhaps, or the path that leads to the rows of workshops—the tannery, the shoemaker's, the blacksmith, and so on. But Micah did not seem too interested in talking with me. He was too busy jumping and humming.

The schoolhouse dog trotted along with us.

"Go back," I said, waving my arms at him. "You can't come with us to the cathedral."

"What's his name?" Micah asked, stooping to pet the floppy-eared dog.

"Felix," I replied. "He's named after a saint, although I don't know which one. There were a lot of Saint Felixes."

"Do you want to dance with me, Felix?" Micah asked, bouncing up and down. The dog bounced with him. Micah began to sing:

Dance, little dog, said the Raven to the Cur,
Dance on your toes and feel the wind in your fur,
Dance and spin 'til the bright day is done,
And me and my lady will join you in the fun.

Micah and Felix danced around and around as Micah sang. I did not dance. I stood still and felt foolish. I hoped no one was looking. When I think back now to the exhibition I made of myself during the Pestilence, it is funny that I felt so embarrassed about Micah's dancing on that day. I did not know then that I could be the person I later became. And I do not know now if I could ever be that person again.

The song had a long number of verses, and when he came to the end, he seemed to be starting up again. I grabbed his arm. "We're supposed to be going to the cathedral," I said.

I suddenly felt the need to impress him. Micah seemed big to me, then, and I wanted to show him something even bigger than himself. I wanted him to be my size, so that I could talk to him.

So I took him to the main door of the cathedral. Generally, we enter the cathedral through the vestry, which opens directly on the chancel, by the choir stalls. Now we would be entering through the nave. It took both my skinny arms to pull open the great oak portal enough for us to go through. I let Micah go in ahead of me, then pulled the door shut behind us.

The cathedral was empty, except for us. Sun came in the windows, laying light and colors on the floor. Wisps of fog, trapped since morning, played and danced high in the dome.

Micah didn't say a word.

He walked, silent on his feet, and seemed to be testing the air of that great vaulted place.

"I come here on my own sometimes," I said, my voice barely above a whisper. "We're not supposed to be in here except for services, but I come anyway. It's a secret," I added, looking at him to see if he understood.

He did not return my look, but there was nothing in his manner to suggest he would betray me.

His eyes found the labyrinth the same time his feet did. I joined him there, and for a while we walked in silence round the pattern on the floor.

"People come here and listen to the singing?" he asked.

"Not just the singing. They listen to the prayers and the sermons too," I said, although people probably do pay more attention to the music. "Haven't you ever been to a church service before?"

"What for? I did try to sleep in a church a few times, when the night was cold, but I always got thrown out. I've sung outside a church, and people gave me money. Is that how it works inside, too?"

"Is that how what works?"

"The money—will people come up and hand me their money, or do I walk around and collect it after I sing?"

My mouth hung open for a long time until I could speak again. "No one gives any money to you. Deacons go through the crowd with their baskets, and people put their offerings in the baskets."

"And then it comes to me? Oh, I know the rest

of the choir will get a bit of it, but most will come to me, because I'm the best singer."

"No, no, you don't understand. You don't get any of the money. God gets it all."

"God gets it? He gets the money for my singing? Where is he? I'd like to talk to him about that." Micah looked around as if God were lurking in the shadows.

"God doesn't get the money directly," I said, struggling to explain something I realized I didn't really understand myself. "The money first goes to Brother Vigor, the treasurer."

"And he gives it to God?"

An organ note sounded from the choir loft. Mercifully, it shut Micah up. More notes followed the first. Micah followed the spiraling sounds first with his head, then, as they came faster and fuller, with his feet. He ran up the aisle to the choir loft.

I, who had never even thought of running in the cathedral, found myself galloping after him.

Brother Paul, the choirmaster, was sitting at the organ. He looked up and smiled at us, and stopped playing. If he had noticed that we'd been running, against the rules, he didn't say anything. He probably didn't notice. He never notices anything but music.

"The new choirboy," he said. "Wonderful. I have not yet heard you sing. Will you sing something for me now?"

I wanted to warn Brother Paul that Micah's songs were not fit for the house of God, but I don't think he would have cared, and I hadn't counted on Micah.

He sang the first note, then stopped in surprise as the note rose to the ceiling and hovered there. His voice sounded different in the cathedral than it did, I think, on the streets of Paris. Then he sang a different note, and his song this time was not about a drunken bishop but told of a woman weeping for the loss of her sons at war. The song, as he sang it, brought an ache to my chest. It made me think of things I do not think about, unless the night is dark and I cannot sleep. It made me long for things I cannot have, and mourn for things that have gone away.

Micah's voice soared like a falcon, and when it was done flying and settled again among the dust of the choir stalls, neither he nor I nor Brother Paul spoke for a long, long moment.

"Try singing this," Brother Paul said, and hummed a Te Deum. "Henri, show him how it's sung."

I haven't a voice like Micah, but I had been singing the Te Deum for many years, and knew it completely. I sang the Te Deum through once, twice, and when I began singing it a third time, Micah joined in. Our voices blended, mine with Micah's, and the song rose like a prayer.

"You will not be a probationer long, I can see that," Brother Paul said. "You will very soon wear a surplice, and if you work hard, we will make you into a solo boy."

This was good news for Micah. When we got back to the schoolhouse, he bragged and he boasted until the choirboys had had enough. Several boys picked him up, hauled him up the stairs to the necessarium, lifted the wooden seat lid, and dumped him down into the pit.

Immediately after, for reasons I could not explain, I jumped in after him.

CHAPTER FIVE

I was engulfed by stink. I flopped around, trying to find my way out, and bumped into Micah, who was trying to do the same. We knocked each other back into the muck.

"Hold still, you idiots! Keep your eyes closed!" I heard Arlo's voice. "And keep your mouths closed, too, if that's possible for you, Micah."

I felt Arlo's grip on my arm and grabbed Micah with the other as Arlo dragged us both out of the pit.

"Now I am covered in muck, too. I'll have to jump in the river with you," he said, as he pulled us stumbling across the green. "What were you thinking of Henri? I can see why they tossed Micah down there, but what possessed you to jump in after him?"

I kept my mouth closed. So did Micah. Arlo took advantage of Micah's enforced silence to lecture him. "You've done a lot of things we haven't done, but we know things that you don't. If you stop behaving like a jackass, maybe we can learn from each other. I don't like idiots in my choir." He kept up the lecture all the way to the river.

The spring current was swift, and the water still held winter's chill. Arlo had a grip on my tunic, but his attention was focused on yelling at Micah and washing the filth off himself.

I bobbed in the river. The coldness of the water surrounded my chest, dragging me down. The current was too strong for me to fight, and the cold kept weighing me down.

Suddenly, I was snatched up. "Oh, no, what have I done?" Arlo wailed. "Pick up his feet," he yelled at Micah. I felt myself floating, as they ran with me to the infirmary.

They were too late, or the water was too cold. My old friend Sickness found me, and I settled once again into the weightlessness of fever.

I spent three days in Limbo, hovering between this world and the next, as if God couldn't make up his mind where he wanted me. That is a familiar place for me.

The threads that tie me to this earth decided to pull me down again from where I floated. On the fourth day, I opened my eyes, and there was Micah, sitting by my bed. He was holding a cloth to his nose. There were spots of blood on it.

"Are you alive?" he asked me.

For a moment, I wasn't sure. "I think so," I said. Then, as more fog lifted, and I could see I was back in my old infirmary bed, with Brother Sebastien tending to other patients nearby, I was able to answer firmly, "Yes, I'm alive."

Brother Sebastien, seeing I was awake, wiped my face with a damp cloth, and helped me drink some water. "Welcome back," he said with a smile.

He took the cloth from Micah's nose and looked at his face. "Another choirboy who will live. Please keep your face away from fists. We don't need choir-boys with black eyes."

He motioned to an assistant, who handed him a bowl of hot broth. "Feed the lad," he said to Micah. "Help him regain his strength. He'll need it, if he is to be your friend."

Micah looked at the bowl and spoon, and looked at me, as if he couldn't figure out how to bring it all together.

Brother Sebastien pushed him gently toward me. "The spoon goes in the mouth," he said, then walked away.

Slowly, carefully, the first spoonful of broth came at me. He seemed surprised that I opened my mouth, and the mission was successful. "This is easy," he said, and fed me some more.

I recognized the flavors of mutton and onion. Brother Sebastien said they built strength. Micah kept spooning it into me until I had enough, then he put the bowl down.

Medicina, the infirmary cat, left ill Brother Roberto, whose feet she was keeping warm, and came over to Micah to inspect this new intruder in her home. She walked all around him, looking and sniffing.

"Hello, kitty," Micah said softly, bending down and stretching out a hand to pet her.

Medicina reared up, arched her back, and hissed angrily at him. Micah drew back and kicked out at her, but she was too fast for him.

"Stupid cat," he muttered, as he watched Medicina curl back around the feet of Brother Roberto.

"Be glad," I said from my bed. "It means you are not going to die."

Micah turned and looked at me.

"Brother Bart found her on one of his wanderings," I said. "Her name is Medicina. It means medicine. She only goes to those who are near death. She was with me until yesterday. She was a comfort, but I was glad to see her go."

"You were going to die?"

"I'm always going to die," I said. "Father Abbot himself gave me the last rites this time. I've had them four times, although not always from Father Abbot. Father Prior did it once—but he didn't seem like his heart was in it."

"I was going to die, too," Micah said. "I was almost hanged. You should have been there. It was so exciting!"

I closed my eyes. I was too weary to listen to bragging.

Micah was quiet for so long, I began to think he'd fallen asleep on the edge of my bed. Then he spoke again.

"It was horrible," he said, in a small voice. "The magistrate didn't even know me. How can he hang someone he doesn't even know? It doesn't seem right. They put me in a cell. It was cold and dark and smelled bad. When Brother Bart came down to get me out, I thought he was the hangman, and I screamed and screamed."

I opened my eyes again. Micah was looking down at the floor, like he was ashamed.

"It's all right," I said. "I get scared sometimes, too."

He got restless, then, and paced around, finally stopping to look out the window.

"You're looking at our special rosebush," Brother Sebastien told him. "It was just a muddy stick when Brother Bart brought it back from one of his wanderings. He gave it to Brother Keith, the gardener, to put in the ground. Brother Keith felt foolish, but he did as he was told, and a few weeks later, we had this lovely rosebush. It blooms longer than any other flowers in the garden."

Medicina meowed then, and Brother Sebastien went over to Brother Roberto, lying on a nearby bed. The cat was no longer warming Brother Roberto's feet.

She was sitting on the bedpost, washing a paw. She hissed at Brother Sebastien when he bent down to check on the sick monk.

"Brother Roberto has been gathered unto God," he said, pulling the sheet over the man's face. He nodded at one of his assistants to inform the other monks. "I did not think he would go so quickly." He knelt by the bed and began his prayers.

Micah sat down beside me. Around us the monks, ill and well, were making the sign of the cross and sending their prayers after Brother Roberto's soul. I saw Micah look at them, then at Medicina.

"That's some cat," he said.

"Everything Brother Bart brings here never looks like much at first, but it turns out to be something special. That's his gift."

Monks swept into the infirmary in the way they have of moving quickly without seeming to be in a hurry. They prepared Brother Roberto for his move to the mourning chapel.

Micah watched them in silence, then said, "Brother Bart brought *me* here." He tossed the thought around in his mind.

Then he smiled.

CHAPTER SIX

I had always been friendly with the other boys. Someone as sickly as me had to be friendly. They, mostly, did not tease me, because of my weakness. They would never have dumped *me* down the necessarium.

I stayed out of their way, except when I was being useful. "Help me with this translation," they'd say, since I am second only to Arlo in Latin, or "Let Henri hold the bets—he's the only one we can trust." But when they thought of friendship, they did not think of me.

Micah thought of me.

I used to think that the boy who would be my friend would share my love of books. I imagined we would discuss philosophy and poetry. My friend turned out to be a boy who was rougher than rough, who couldn't read a word, and would sooner balance a book on his head during a dance than learn what was inside.

He came to see me regularly. He'd pop into the infirmary when I knew he was supposed to be in

Latin class or choir practice. "Are you well yet?" he'd ask, flopping himself down on my bed.

We'd talk and laugh, getting more and more boisterous until Brother Sebastien threw him out. Even after that, Micah would stand at the window, pulling faces to make me laugh, and acting out little windowpane dramas, which chiefly consisted of him hitting himself on the head. Brother Sebastien would have to draw the shutters to make me rest.

"It's not fair," Micah said one day. "I was brought here to sing, but I'm not allowed to sing until I know Latin. What will I do with Latin?"

"It's the language of the Church."

"I won't be singing to the church. I'll be singing to people."

"You'll be singing to God."

"God can listen if he wants to, but why can't he speak a sensible language like French?"

"I can teach you the Latin words," I told Micah. "You can learn what they sound like without knowing what they mean. We sing the same things over and over again, anyway." I ticked them off on my fingers. "Show us mercy, glory to God, take away our sin, God is holy, give us peace..."

"I know songs that are much more entertaining," Micah said.

"Mass isn't supposed to be entertaining," I said.

"Why not?"

I tried to explain, but I was not successful. It didn't help that, in the middle of my explanation, Micah noticed a large fly hovering over the face of a monk sleeping nearby. The fly landed on the monk's nose, and the monk wiggled his face in his sleep to shake it off.

When the fly flew right into the monk's open, snoring mouth, it was too much for us, and we collapsed with laugher. Micah laughed louder than me—I felt a twinge of guilt, laughing at a monk—but Brother Sebastien told us both to be quiet. He sent Micah away, and told me to go to sleep. He was gruff and stern, but I saw he was trying hard not to smile.

In the days that followed, I taught Micah to sing the Kyrie and the rest of the sung Eucharist. He learned quickly, and was soon promoted to the full choir. The sick monks smiled at our singing, although they smiled wider when Micah sang one of his street songs.

I was glad to finally be released from the infirmary a fortnight later. The spring evening was both cool and warm, washing my face with a light mist. I liked the feel of the muscles stretching in my legs as I took long strides across the green, and I was happy to be leaving the sick world behind. After all, I had a friend waiting for me in the schoolhouse.

I opened the schoolhouse door and saw Micah, standing on the refectory table, giving an impression of the Prior saying Mass.

He mimicked the Prior perfectly, the way the Prior seemed to look down his nose at everyone, his strutting around the altar, his impatience with the choirboys who served at the altar with him. He was the Prior, exactly.

He saw me at the door, stopped staggering, and hopped down from the table.

"You're back!" he exclaimed, and drew me to the table. "Look who's back, everyone!" He grabbed Oswin's mug, filled it with ale, and handed it to me.

"Stop hogging the bread," he said to Gaston, grabbing the end of a loaf and a hunk of cheese and pushing these at me as well. "Well, say hello, everyone," Micah joked.

Obediently, they did, all of them, and seemed surprised that they were doing so.

Micah launched into one of his street songs, and the other boys, even Arlo, joined in. This was not a song they would have learned in the abbey. Micah must have taught them, the way he had taught me a song or two. But not this one. This song had a great many actions that could be done with it, and all the other boys knew them. They were all sitting and waving their arms, and laughing while they sang.

And I just sat. I could have tried to learn the song. I could have enjoyed it and joined in, in some fashion, even if I got it all wrong. That is what I would do now.

But then, it was easier to feel sorry for myself than to change my ways. Fate had put me outside of things, and there I would stay, alone. Micah clearly had other friends. I left them to their singing, climbed the stairs to the dormitory, and went to bed.

I woke up in the middle of the night. When I was unable to fall back to sleep, I decided to visit the scriptorium. I quietly dressed, and tiptoed out of the dormitory, carrying my sandals until I got downstairs.

There are two ways to get to the cathedral and the main buildings. One way is across the green. The other is underground. Tunnels and passageways, secret and well-known, travel to every corner of the abbey, including the schoolhouse. I took a tallow candle, lit it from the embers in the refectory fireplace, and went down the winding stairs into the tunnel.

I followed the tunnel from the schoolhouse, past where it branched off to the storehouse, kitchen, bathhouse, and monks' dormitory. When I reached the crypt, I heard footsteps behind me.

The crypt is an unnerving place even during the daytime, when some light from the cathedral above filters through. At nighttime, with just a candle, the shadows of the carved figures on top of the coffins were even more menacing.

I stopped, and the footsteps stopped. I moved on, and heard them again.

"Henri," a voice whispered, hoarsely. "What are

you doing out of bed?"

I almost dropped the candle. "Who's there?" I quavered.

"I am a ghost. Whoooo!"

"Don't hurt me!"

The ghost giggled. "I won't hurt you," a boy's voice said, and, of course, it was Micah. "Just tell me where you're going."

"I will not," I said, angry to have been frightened. I raised my candle. "Where are you?"

"Find me," he challenged.

"We can't play in here," I said. "We'll get into trouble."

"I'm always in trouble. What are they going to do—hang us?" He laughed, and I thought I heard him moving, but everything echoes down in the crypt, and I couldn't be sure.

"Stop fooling around. Where are you?"

"Right here," he said, suddenly popping up in front of me.

I let out a whoop, and nearly dropped the candle again.

"Who's down there?" a voice called down from the sacristy.

It was Brother Pascal, in the cathedral to prepare for the night service. I grabbed Micah and ran all the way to the scriptorium.

At the entrance, I paused. Not for fear of discovery—

with the monks at their prayers, I knew it would be empty. Micah started in, but I put my hand out and stopped him. This was my territory.

"Shhh," I whispered. "Listen."

Micah managed to stay still and silent for slightly longer than an instant, then asked, "What are we listening for?"

"All the people who wrote these books. Sometimes I can hear them talking to me."

"The books talk to you?"

"They whisper to me," I said. "They tell me I can learn their secrets. They tell me I can become one of them."

"And you want that?"

"I want that." I reached out a hand and stroked the nearest book. The sacristan can have his gold cross and silver chalice. Books, to me, are the real sacred objects.

I knew Micah didn't understand that, any more than I understood his habit of dancing on tabletops. But it didn't matter.

In other monasteries, the scriptorium and the library are separate. At St. Luc's, they are combined in one big room, filled with desks and books, with anterooms and alcoves filled with even more books. Micah wandered around, the full moon shining in the windows.

"Can you read all these books?"

"Most of them," I said. "There are some in alphabets I can't read yet, but I will one day."

"Will you read them to me sometime?"

"Why don't I teach you to read? Then you can read them for yourself."

"Why do I need to learn to read if you'll do my reading for me?"

"Everyone in here reads."

"Well, no one out there reads, and they all seem to manage just fine." Micah jerked his thumb out the window, in the direction of the world beyond the wall.

That there could be anyone who didn't want to know how to read was such a new thought to me that I could not think of anything to say.

I took Micah back to the schoolhouse. As we passed through the crypt, we could hear the monks chanting overhead. A little further on, we smelled the morning bread baking. We snuck into the bakery—easy to do, with the monks all in Chapel—and snatched some fresh rolls off the cooling trays. We munched them as we crossed the green, getting our feet wet in the cold dew on the grass. Felix, the schoolhouse dog, ran out to greet us, putting his wet paws all over our tunics.

We played together all the time after that. I never knew how much fun having fun could be. I never imagined that I could enjoy trying to hop around the cloisters on one foot, or sneaking up to the top of the bell tower, or catching fish in the river and frying them up in the schoolhouse fireplace, or chasing the young pigs around the pig pen. Even the crypt lost some of its mystery after Micah and I invented Ghost Jump, a sort of silent hide-and-seek game we invited the other boys to play with us there. It became very popular, our game. I suspect choirboys here will still be playing it long after the current crop is gone.

On rainy days, we'd walk the labyrinth in the cathedral. We could hear the rain falling on the vaulted roof, high above us. With light flickering from the altar candles, we walked round and round the labyrinth pattern worked into the floor of the nave. By now, Micah knew the church music and was a choirboy proper, even singing solos. He would begin to sing, and I would answer, the way the choir and monks sing back and forth to each other during service. Our voices soared high in the rafters, mixing with the sound of raindrops, and we moved as if in a dream.

I played with Micah and the others, I studied hard, and sang at services. I forgot all about the desperate man with his tale of death, but all the while the Plague was getting closer and closer, a great, hungry, stalking animal, swallowing up everything in its path.

CHAPTER SEVEN

Now that I have begun this chronicle, I wish I could do nothing else with my time until the story is done, but that is not possible. I'm still a choirboy, and it is still my job to sing at services. It's even more important now, with fewer choirboys than before, and fewer monks. The sound we make is thinner, and if God is listening, he will have to strain to hear us.

By the time this chronicle is found, there will be all new monks at St. Luc's. The ones I know now, and knew before the Calamity, will all be gone. The loftier monks will be in the crypt where the choirboys play Ghost Jump. The ordinary monks will be buried in the cemetery outside, their graves marked only by a small, white cross.

I shall be dead, too, most likely, and buried somewhere in the abbey. Will I have a carved stone tomb in the crypt, or a plain white cross in the field? I doubt that I shall care, when the time comes.

There were over two hundred monks here when

Micah came to St. Luc's. There are scarcely half that now. We lost Brother Beltran, the Latin master. (There was some rejoicing at this in the schoolhouse—Brother Beltran was constantly grumpy, and the only thing he seemed to enjoy about boys was hitting them with his palmer. But I learned much from him, and wept at his death.)

Brother Nestor, the cobbler, and Brother Probus, the assistant sacristan, were also taken by the Plague, and so many others.

Brother Paul the choirmaster is still with us. His head is so full of music there was no room for the Pestilence to settle there. Brother Joel, the chief sculptor, who can turn a piece of marble into a saint overnight, is still here, as is Brother Joseph, the abbey's inventor.

Brother Marc likewise escaped the Plague. He is the abbey's chief illuminator, and always has a blotch of paint on his nose. Micah and I and the others spent a lot of time watching him draw funny pictures and paint glorious designs on the manuscripts other monks copied out. He let us try our hand at illuminating. Neither Micah nor I showed any gift for that, although Garwood did, which was surprising, since he was such a rough boy.

I am closest to Brother Sebastien, not a surprise, since I have spent so much time in his care. Even when I am not ill, I spend time in his laboratory, mixing herbs and learning his secrets.

Brother Kenneth, in charge of the abbey's wine, had a great, booming voice, and a laugh that was even more robust than Brother Bart's. He had big muscles from moving casks of wine, and loved to play rough games with the rough boys. He often arrived at his seat in Chapel sweaty and out of breath from a game of football before prayers. He would have been great at Ghost Jump if he hadn't been a monk. But all Brother Kenneth's strength did not defend him from the Plague.

The Plague did not take the Prior. He was so unpleasant the Plague Monster would have gulped him down and spit him right out again.

"We call him the Pickle," I told Micah, "because he's always so sour."

I don't know why he became a monk—if he had any of the necessary qualities, only God knew about them. The Prior didn't like choirboys, he didn't like the other monks, and, as far as I could tell, he didn't even like God.

He did like being Prior, though. He liked wearing the most luxurious robes for Mass. I know this because Micah and I, spying on him, often caught him standing in front of the mirror in the monks' vestry, posing in his vestments. It was quite funny.

Micah pulled a wonderful trick on him one day. I helped, but it was his idea.

Micah and I were in the herbarium one day. I was sweeping the floor for Brother Sebastien. Micah was wandering around the hut, looking at everything. He lifted every jar of herbs, examining, smelling and tasting.

"These aren't poison, are they?" he asked.

"Brother Sebastien keeps the poisonous herbs under lock," I assured him, so he kept nosing around while I did the sweeping.

"Oh! Oh, this is horrible!" Micah's face was contorted, as he spat out the taste in his mouth onto the floor.

"I just swept there!"

"What an awful-tasting herb! Imagine a plant tasting that bad! Here—you try it."

"Why would you want me to taste something you say is so vile? I'm sure it will taste the same to my tongue as it did to yours."

"Henri, it's too nasty to be believed. You must taste it, to see if I'm right."

I gave in, and put a pinch of the dried, ground herbs on my tongue. My spit soon joined Micah's on the floor, but still I could not rid my mouth of the taste.

"What foul stuff!" I found some mint for us to chew on to sweeten our tongues, then went back to sweeping.

"Henri?"

"Do you want some more mint? Help yourself."

He shook his head. He was sitting on the chopping table, running his fingers through the bitter herb in the pot. "How do you think this would mix with wine?"

I stopped sweeping. "Micah, you can't do that! Brother Kenneth is a friend!"

"I wasn't thinking of the general abbey wine. I was thinking of the communion wine. That's Brother Pascal's responsibility, isn't it?"

Brother Pascal, the sacristan, in charge of the sacred objects used in the cathedral, never had a kind word for the choirboys.

"Haven't you ever noticed what a big swallow of wine the Prior takes at communion?" Micah asked. I thought for a moment, then a smile took over my whole face.

Once we'd made certain of when next the Prior was presiding, getting the bitter herb into the communion wine was only a matter of speeding through the catacombs before the sung Eucharist. The jug of wine was already on the altar. Adding the herb, swirling it around in the wine, then disappearing into the crypt before we could be discovered was easy.

"Watch the Prior's face, but don't give anything away," we told the other boys. Arlo looked like he wanted to ask a question, but thought better of it and said nothing.

It took great self-restraint to keep still during the

service. Finally, the prayer over the wine was said, and the Prior raised the chalice to his lips. He took a big drink.

He went green. His lips puckered up, then twisted around his face as that awful taste spread through his mouth. His eyes bulged out and began to water, and his whole face contorted. He couldn't spit the wine out—it was sacred, after all. He had to actually swallow the foul mixture.

In the choir, we kept our faces blank as the Prior mangled his way through the Benedictio. We saved our laughter for the vestry and the schoolhouse, afterward.

Of all the monks, Brother Bart was the one Micah most took to. I'd see them walking together around the inside of the abbey walls, Brother Bart trying to tame his wandering feet. Sometimes I joined them, but mostly I let them walk on their own. They had both lived out in the world, and had stories to share that did not concern me.

"He used to be a soldier," Micah told me. "He walked away in the middle of a battle."

"Was he afraid?"

"I asked him that, and he said no. He said he had killed a lot of men that day, and was just raising his sword to kill another when he realized he didn't know why he was killing him. He had no quarrel with that man, or with any of the men on the battlefield, and decided right then and there that he was never going to kill someone again. So he dropped his sword, unhooked his armor, and walked away from the battle. And no one hurt him, even though there were men still fighting all around. Isn't that strange?"

"Why did he become a monk?"

"He said he thought he could find answers that way. I told him it must be much more exciting to be a soldier than a monk, and he said the excitement of a battle lasts only a moment, but the excitement of understanding lasts forever."

"And what did you say?"

"I told him I didn't understand, and he laughed and we kept walking."

I had never thought to ask such questions of a monk. I had lived my entire life with nuns and monks. I accepted their ways the same as I accept the sun rising and the rain falling. But to Micah, they were strange creatures, whose customs were nonsensical or downright foolish. His questions opened doors in my mind I hadn't thought were there.

And even though I had lived at St. Luc's for many years, once Micah began exploring the tunnels, he found secret doors and passageways even I had not discovered. He especially enjoyed the tunnels and staircases that led to the monks' quarters, a place forbidden to choirboys.

"It's Chapter House time," Micah would say,

pulling me out of the vestry after service. Into the tunnels we'd go, coming up behind a secret door of the chapter house. Every morning, monks gathered in this bright, round room to discuss abbey business. Micah and I would listen and watch, and then I would be late for class.

Many times, I woke to Micah shaking me. "It's matins." Sometimes he went on his own when I would not be roused, but generally I went with him. Up into the cathedral balcony we'd creep, high against the arches, and lie on our bellies, looking down at the sleepy monks chanting the early morning service.

"What would happen if we dropped something on the Pickle's head?" Micah whispered to me one night, as we looked down on a chapel full of round bald spots.

"It depends on what we dropped. If we dropped a feather, no one would care. If we dropped an anvil, we'd be singing at his funeral mass. Requiescat in pace."

"Requiem for a Pickle," Micah said. I started giggling and had to wiggle quickly out of the balcony.

Then there was the trick with the pig.

The monks were celebrating one of the saint's days with a special feast after compline. Several dignitaries, including the Bishop, were guests. The centerpiece of this fine meal was to be several roasted suckling pigs.

When the monks were on their way to service, we crept into the kitchen and replaced one of the roasted pigs with a live one, full of wine and sleeping. Then we ran through the catacombs, robing just in time to take our places in the choir.

After service, we stood outside the monks' refectory, to watch the fun through the windows.

The platters of food were all on the tables, including the four covered pig platters. The monks and their guests had not yet begun to eat. The Bishop was giving one of his very long speeches.

"Which is our pig?" Micah asked.

I couldn't tell. Then I saw something move, and nudged my friend. We watched in fascination as the dome over one of the platters began to jiggle.

One by one, the brothers turned their attention from the Bishop to the strange behavior of the serving dish. The Bishop finally realized that no one was paying the slightest bit of attention to him, and he, in turn, stared at the platter. By now, the lid was banging, and strange squealing noises were coming from inside.

Brother Simon was the first to react. As kitchener, he was responsible for the meal. Leaning between Brothers Bernard and Anthony, he reached across the table and lifted the dancing lid off the platter.

Our pig blinked at the sudden light, then jumped off the platter, running madly down the length of the table, scattering platters of vegetables and mugs of ale. When he came to the end, he took a great leap, and landed in the lap of the Prior.

Micah and I dropped to the ground, laughing, our hands clamped over our mouths to keep the noise inside.

Later that night, we snuck out of the dormitory and went down to a corner of the storehouse, where we had hidden the roasted pig. We tore great chunks of cold pork off the roast, and ate with abandon.

"Did you see the look on the Pickle's face when the pig landed in his lap?" Micah asked, tossing aside a bone.

We laughed at the memory. "We should have taken some cider to wash this down," I said.

"Here you are, boys." Brother Bart handed us a jug.

I jumped up and foolishly tried to hide the hunk of roast pork behind my back.

Micah stayed seated. He grabbed hold of the jug, took a great swallow, and laughed and laughed, his mouth full of pork and sweet cider dripping down his chin. It was a moment of pure joy, and Brother Bart and I had no choice but to join in.

We spent our free time the next day cleaning out the pigpen. Brother Bart never told the other monks on us, though. I know he didn't. He is that sort of monk.

CHAPTER EIGHT

I was able to see Paris before the Calamity began.

Brother Paul made an announcement at the beginning of choir practice one morning late in May.

"We have been chosen to sing at the opening of the Lendit Fair in Paris in June. This will mean extra rehearsals, but it is a great honor, and long overdue. It is many years since St. Luc's performed there."

He went on to talk about what we would sing, and how the monks from other abbeys would join us in the grand procession, but I stopped listening. I had never been outside the abbey walls, not once since arriving at St. Luc's.

I became hot and cold all at once, both excited and scared. I wanted to beg to be left behind, and I couldn't wait to go. A fair! I could not even begin to imagine what that was.

The other boys, more wordly than I, were simply excited. We talked about it afterward in the vestry. We were hanging up our surplices, but keeping our cassocks on, as we'd be right back in the cathedral after class.

All except Micah, that is. He didn't attend classes anymore. Brother Beltran had reached his limit, and now Brother Bart had the task of keeping Micah busy while the rest of us were at school. Brother Bart found him little jobs with the other monks, helping out in the workshops. He was much happier, and Brother Beltran was happier, and I concentrated again in class, but I missed him.

"People come from all over," Micah told us. "I've been many times. People sell things there that the rest of you boys, with your tiny little lives, can't even imagine. And the entertainment! Jugglers and mummers and dancers from strange places. Of course, I always made more money than everyone else, because I'm more talented than everyone else."

"Oh, stop it," Gaston said. "Ever since you've become a solo boy, you've become unbearable."

"He was unbearable before," Arlo reminded Gaston. "Pay no attention to him. Even if what he says is half true, it doesn't matter. We won't be able to see any of it. You heard Brother Paul. It's to be a procession. We won't have a chance to see anything."

"Lucky for you, isn't it, Micah? You won't have to prove your claim," Garwood taunted. "I'll bet everything you've told us about your life in Paris is a lie. If anyone threw anything at you when you sang, it was probably mud, not coins."

"Brother Paul thinks Micah has a good voice,"

young Rafe piped up.

"Brother Paul has beeswax in his ears," Oswin chimed in.

"I haven't told you one single lie," Micah said, hotly, which I knew to be a lie, but so what?

"Prove it," Bayard challenged. "Prove that you're more than hot air."

"And how do you expect me to do that?"

"Come back from Paris with a purse full of money," Antoine said, joining in the dare. "For a singer as famous as you, it should be easy."

"And if you don't, we'll know you're a liar, and we'll drop you down the necessarium again."

"And if I do, you'll all have to bow down before me in the cathedral," Micah said.

"No messing about in the cathedral," Arlo said. "Think of something else."

The boys thought for a moment. "I know," Hugh said. "If Micah comes back from Paris with a pouch full of money, we'll make him Boy Bishop on St. Nicholas Day."

"I was going to be Boy Bishop this year!" Gaston protested.

"And so you will be," Arlo said. "Micah won't have a chance to earn a single coin at the fair, much less a whole purseful. And you," he turned to me, sternly, "when they dump your friend down the necessarium, I'm going to tie you to a chair so you can't jump in after him again. Now, line up for class."

As we headed across the green, Micah grabbed my arm. "What's the Boy Bishop?"

"Every year on St. Nicholas Day in December, one of us is elected Boy Bishop."

"A bishop. I'd like that." He grinned at me. "Don't worry—I'll be the Boy Bishop, *and* I'll show you the fair." He dashed off to find Brother Bart, and I hurried off to class.

Monks from other abbeys began arriving a few days before the fair opened. Micah and I helped out the kitchen monks, harried by so many more mouths to feed.

"The Bishop is coming today," Brother Simon told us, looking worried. "I hope we've prepared enough food. The higher up they are in the Church, the more they like to eat." He looked even more worried when he realized he'd spoken his criticism out loud, but Micah and I could keep a secret.

On the morning of the first day of the fair, we lined up in a great procession for the three-mile journey into Paris. We wore clean cassocks and stiff, bright surplices.

"This is a holy procession," the Prior lectured to us before we set out. "We will be carrying the most important relic in our reliquary, a piece of the True Cross. Your behavior must uphold the solemnity of the occasion." He frowned most particularly at

Micah and myself. This was, perhaps justified, but still impolite.

Our two lines of choirboys were flanked on each side by priests, friars, and monks from our abbey and from other abbeys and orders. In addition to the black robes of the Benedictines, there were the gray robes of the Franciscans, the white of the Cistercians, and the black-and-white garb of the Dominicans. Monks had been arriving at St. Luc's for days in preparation for the opening of the fair. Services sung by that many voices had been exhilarating.

The Bishop was with us on this procession. He was being carried there in his decorated litter. I felt sorry for the monks carrying him, bending under his great weight.

When everyone was in place, we set out. At first, it wasn't much fun, walking slowly down the road, chanting plainsong. Soon, though, it became interesting, as villagers and peasants lined the pathways to see the procession. Many kneeled as we went by. It made me feel important, and I walked a little taller and tried to look holy.

A group of people were very wretched-looking in sad rags that covered their limbs and faces. Some of them held out baskets at the end of long poles. Others carried small bells or clackers.

"Who are they?" I asked Micah. He was walking next to me.

"Lepers," Micah replied. "They ring bells to keep people away, and their begging bowls are on poles so that people can give them alms without getting too close." I saw Micah looking at boys our age, dressed in rags, the way he had been when he first came to the abbey. I could not tell what he was thinking. I never remembered to ask him.

The quiet countryside gave way to the bustle of Paris. Outside the city walls were camps for the trading of horses and cattle. Piles of firewood and vegetables were being loaded into peddlers' carts. There were people everywhere—beggars, merchants, farm people and city people, and some whose appearance was so strange to me, they might have come from a dream.

We walked through the gates and into the heart of the market. The crowd parted for us as the Red Sea parted for Moses, people bowing and crossing themselves as we passed by.

I, who had never been in the world beyond the abbey walls, was overwhelmed with sensation. The sights, the noise, the smells! Open sewers ran down the center of the street. People shouted and moved without order. I saw a dead donkey rotting on a street corner, with big black rats scrambling over it. I saw men wearing velvets and big hats with peacock feathers, and urchins in rags fighting over scraps of garbage someone tossed out a window.

The confusion scared me, and I wanted to rush back behind my walls. I turned to Micah, and he was so clearly enjoying himself that I stopped being afraid, and began to enjoy myself, too.

We joined the Bishop, the Prior, and a number of very important-looking clerics on a large platform in the center of the fair. We sang the Te Deum and several introits that had solos for Micah. He sang as if his mind was on the music, not our escape.

From the platform, we could look out across the fair, and see what we were missing. There were jugglers, a puppet show, and a group of tumblers. A tightrope walker performed next to a band of pipers and drummers. In every available space, people bought and sold goods of more variety than I ever imagined. I was so excited, I couldn't keep still, and I lost my place in the psalm several times.

At long last, the blessing was completed, and the benediction was sung. Micah kept a grip on my arm as we left the platform. As soon as he saw his chance, he ducked out of the procession, pulling me with him. We watched from our hiding place to be sure we hadn't been seen, then raced away.

"Freedom!" we cried out.

The plan was to see as much as we could, then run back to the abbey, to catch up with the procession before one of the monks realized we were gone. The procession was going to wind its way to several holy sites on the way back to the abbey, so I thought we had a chance.

"Come on!" Micah urged, but I needed no prompting.

Such things we saw! Great tusks of ivory, pearls from the sea, many colors of silk from China, and bolts of fabric woven in Italy. Carpet merchants from Persia spread their elaborate rugs out for the buyers to see, rugs so beautiful I could not imagine putting my feet on them.

In the spice market, huge bowls of spices filled the air with the fragrances of cinnamon, ginger, and cloves. Other spices were for medicine, like the herbs in Brother Sebastien's laboratory.

Every street led to a new wonder, and Micah knew them all.

We went to the parchment market, on the left bank of the river, full of black-robed university students. They were buying parchment so they could copy out the books they needed for their studies.

"Arlo will be one of those soon," I said to Micah.

"I won't be," Micah replied, which made me laugh.

"Gardey-loo!"

The call came from the window above us. In a flash, Micah yanked me away. The woman at the window emptied a full chamberpot into the street. The nasty contents missed us completely, but the people behind us weren't so lucky. They cursed and cursed and we laughed and laughed.

We saw acrobats and jugglers, a dancing bear, a man with a trained monkey, and dancers from foreign lands. If the crowd didn't like a performer, they'd pelt him with swan bones and peach pits.

"Time to go to work," Micah said. I was shy, but he gripped my arm and pulled me with him onto the steps of a building. He began singing, songs I knew, and he was having such a good time, I found myself singing with him.

We must have looked peculiar, two choirboys in cassock and surplice, singing rude street songs, but the crowd cheered for more every time we finished a song. They tossed coins at us which Micah scooped up almost before they landed on the ground.

"Perfect—here comes a pie-man," Micah said.

We exchanged some of our coins for a game pie and a berry pie, both of which we broke apart with our hands and shared. The berries stained our surplices, but we didn't care.

We went to the bird market. "It's called the Vale of Wretchedness," Micah said. "Listen!"

The air was filled with the cries of birds being slaughtered—swans, geese, chickens, pigeons, larks— all kinds. They clucked and chirped in their cages and pens, and squawked and screamed when they were grabbed for the slaughter. Their blood ran free in the square, smelly and sticking under our feet. Alongside the rows of dead birds were displays of hedgehogs, rabbits, and squirrels.

The noise was distressing, and I was glad when Micah led me away and into another square. This one was much more pleasant. The scent of roasting meat was quite agreeable, even though I knew that what was on the grills had come from the wretched square we'd just left. Other food was sold here, too—great round cheeses, loaves of bread, and candied fruit.

"Raisins from Damascus!" the peddlers cried.

"The best onions in Paris!"

"Salmon from the waters of Scotland!"

"I was arrested here," Micah told me. "I tried to steal a skewer of larks off one of these grills. Let's see if we can find the man who had me arrested."

I pulled Micah away. I didn't know what he would want to do if he found the man, but whatever it was, it was certain to mean trouble. We were having too much fun for that.

A man walked near us, selling amulets off a tray. "Protection against the Plague!" he called. "Get your magic amulets, guaranteed to protect you from the Pestilence that is coming!"

"We need one of those," I told Micah.

We went over for a closer look. The amulets were triangles of stiff parchment on thin strips of leather. They were meant to be worn around the neck. On the parchment was the word Abracadabra, written over and over down to a point.

"My magic amulet will keep you alive when everyone around you is dead," the peddler said. "The Plague is coming! The Plague is coming!"

"Should we buy one?" I asked Micah.

"I have a better idea," Micah said. "Can you remember the letters?"

I stared at them until I had them memorized, just before the peddler moved on.

We suddenly realized how late it was getting, and took off running through the city and out the gates.

By a miracle, we reached the tail end of the procession just as it was turning into the abbey. We were sweaty and berry-stained, and of course we got into trouble. We got a stern lecture from the Abbot, another one from the Prior, and we had to spend our free time working in the laundry for the next week.

Micah didn't care. He jangled the coins in front of the choirboys and sang, "I'm the next Boy Bishop!"

I didn't care, either, especially when Gaston said grudgingly to Micah, "All right, all right, you and Henri are brave. You don't need to go on and on about it." No one had ever called me brave before.

Plus, I have a memory of Paris full of color, light, and laughter. In rare, lucky moments, that is the image of the great city that comes to me in the night, not the dreadful place it was soon to become.

I am returning to this chronicle after staying away from it for several days.

I told myself I wanted to concentrate on my studies instead. I have been promoted to the study of the seven arts—grammar, rhetoric, logic, arithmetic, geometry, astronomy, and music—and there is much to learn.

But that was not the reason. The reason is that I do not look forward to remembering and writing down all that came next. I would rather keep remembering the fun, the easy days before the Plague, when the problems we had were all small and simple. There is much more I could write about our games and tricks, but I did not take up this chronicle just to write about the good times.

So, now I continue.

I remember the day everything changed.

Micah and I were headed down to the chapter house after service. We went through the tunnels to the secret door. As was our custom, we opened the door just a crack, to be able to see and hear what was going on.

We were not surprised to hear the Prior complaining about Micah. He usually complained about something during Chapter House, and often, that something was Micah.

This time, he included me.

"He is leading Henri astray," the Prior said. "Every disruption in this abbey since that urchin came to stay has had the two of them behind it. That boy is a devil, a demon, and has no place in our community."

Micah nudged me. He put his fingers behind his head like two horns and bared his teeth. I looked away so I wouldn't laugh.

"Henri is an orphan, and our ward," Brother Marc said.

"But we have no duty to Micah," the Prior said, flatly.

"'I was without shelter, and you took me in,'" Brother Bart said.

"How dare you quote Scripture to me!" The Prior was so angry we could see his nostrils flare, even from across the room.

"Micah is special," Brother Bart insisted. "He must stay!"

The Abbot was listening to the exchange. He looked like he was about to speak when a novice entered the chapter house and walked up to him. He bowed, then spoke into the Abbot's ear.

The Abbot look surprised, then dismayed, as he nodded for the novice to leave.

Father Abbot rose to his feet. The other monks also stood up.

"Both boys are with us to stay," he said. "There will be no more discussion about this. I have just been given grave news to impart to you, my brothers. Word has just been given to me that the Plague has arrived in Paris."

Micah quietly shut the door. We went up to the top of the bell tower, another place where we weren't supposed to be, and looked out at the world. The world looked the same as it always did. The sun was shining, the cows were grazing in the abbey fields, and the air smelled morning-sweet.

We stayed up there for a long time, looking out from the tower.

"Well," Micah finally said, "I wonder what happens now."

At first, the Pestilence arriving in Paris brought very few changes to our lives. The rhythm of abbey life was designed by St. Benedict to continue, unchanging, no matter what was going on in the world outside the walls. The bells still rang, marking the sacred hours and calling the monks to prayer. We choirboys still sang in the cathedral, studied Virgil and Ovid and grammar in Latin class, helped the monks at their labors, and had what fun we could.

The harvest needed to come in. The morning Latin class was canceled so we could help pick fruit and bring in vegetables. The brothers worked at threshing grain until very late at night. Grapes were crushed with bare feet in big vats for Brother Kenneth's wine cellar. Brother Jude the cellarer organized the great stores of food that would see the abbey through the winter.

Along with their work with the harvest, the monks spent more time in Chapel, saying prayers about the Plague. Extra Masses were added to the daily schedule, with extra singing and serving for us. More villagers than usual left their fields around the abbey to come to Mass.

"This is the third Mass today," Oswin complained, as we put on our surplices again in the vestry. "It would be all right in wintertime, if it got us out of Latin class, but the weather is still good."

"Who wants to be in a cathedral when the sun is shining," added Garwood.

"Shut up, both of you," Arlo said. "We'd all rather be fishing or playing ball, but we weren't asked, and we're not likely to be. Now line up, it's time to go in. And no talking in the Sanctuary. You were chattering like magpies this morning."

It was the choirmaster who intervened for us with the Abbot. "You boys need to be out in the fresh air," he told us. "Father Abbot has given me permission to use only half of you at most Masses. We will have the full choir for special services only." Half the choir took one day, giving the others a rest, then we switched around.

Because we felt safe from the Plague behind the high abbey walls we could enjoy scaring ourselves about it in the dormitory at night.

"It will be so horrible, even the trees will bleed," Micah said.

"Trees have no blood," Arlo injected. "Pay no attention to Micah. He doesn't know anything."

"I know more than you," Micah insisted. "I've lived in the world. You spend all your time with monks. There may be things they haven't taught you."

There was no defense to that, so Arlo did not offer one.

"What is this Plague?" Rafe, the youngest of us, asked.

"It's a monster, like in the Revelation," said Gaston. "It's got the tail of a scorpion and breathes fire. It goes from town to town, gobbling up all the idiots."

"You'd better watch out, Rafe. You are just what he's hungry for!"

"You are *all* idiots," Arlo said. "I'll be glad to finally leave here and go to university, where people have intelligence."

"If you're so smart, what is the Plague then?"

"I know the answer to that," I said. "Brother Sebastien told me. It's caused by the planets. Saturn, Jupiter, and Mars appeared together in the sky three years ago. They caused a big earthquake, and poisonous air was released from inside the earth. The bad air carries the Pestilence."

"If it's in the air, how can we avoid it?"

"It won't hurt monks or religious people," I said with certainty.

"But we're not monks."

"We'll be protected by the monks' prayers, those of us who are worthy, that is," Joris said pompously, then "Oww!" as Micah's sandal hit him in the head.

"Henri and I can protect you from the Plague," Micah announced.

Laughter came from several parts of the dormitory.

"You have some special powers, do you?" Arlo asked, sarcastically.

"When we were at the Lendit Fair, we came across a genuine Plague repellent, but since you laughed at us tonight, we won't tell you about it. Soon Henri and I will be the only ones alive in the choir. It's a good thing I sing so well."

The boys jeered and went to sleep. Micah and I

stayed up late, whispering together and making plans.

The next day, Micah and I went into the Plague-amulet business. He rounded up pieces of hemp string to tie them with, and I scrounged pieces of parchment and extra ink from Brother Marc. I cut small triangles of parchment, and wrote "Abracadabra" on them, over and over, down to the point.

I made the amulets, and Micah sold them.

By the end of the day, we were the new owners of Oswin's dice, Bayard's deck of cards, Gaston's cap with the feather in it, Antoine's woolen leggings, a new quill pen from Arlo, and Hugh's pair of stilts.

"What happens if your magic amulet doesn't work?" Hugh asked, reluctantly handing over his stilts. He had been practicing with them for weeks, and could walk a dozen steps without falling off. "What if I die anyway?"

"If the amulet doesn't work, we'll give you the stilts back," Micah said.

Hugh was satisfied with that guarantee. Micah handed him an amulet. Hugh put it around his neck, and slipped it under his tunic.

"We'd better not let the monks see these," Arlo said. "They wouldn't like them. They're not exactly religious."

"Abracadabra makes as much sense to me as the prayers we say at Mass," Micah said.

Arlo's eyes widened with shock. "It's a good

thing God smiles on fools, Micah." Then he turned to me and said, "Don't let this simpleton repeat that where anybody can hear him. It's blasphemy. He's already escaped the executioner once. I don't think he'd be so lucky a second time."

CHAPTER TEN

O

ut of the shadows of the night, and into a shaft of moonlight, a procession was making its way up the road to the abbey. We watched it come closer.

Micah had shaken me awake. The strange sounds we heard made us sneak out of the dormitory and run across the green to the front wall. Micah helped me climb to the top, and we strained our eyes to see into the darkness.

"Who are they?" I asked Micah. "They're chanting, but they're not monks." There were men, women, and children in the procession, dressed in the sort of clothes that monks gave up when they became monks. The men wore doublets and hose, with cloaks hooked over their shoulders. The ladies wore cloaks and gowns and garments I can't even name, having had very limited experience of women.

"They're not beggars, either." We could see that the clothes they wore were not rags.

"They are pilgrims, going on pilgrimage," the Abbot said, coming up behind us and making us jump out of our skins. "And you are going back to bed. Don't worry—they will still be here in the morning."

"I wish he wouldn't creep up on us," Micah said, as we ran back to the schoolhouse. "A decent abbot would give us a chance to hide."

We planned to get up before dawn, but we slept in until breakfast. The others had the news before we did.

"It's Gaston's father, the marquis," Oswin said. "He's going on pilgrimage to see the Pope in Avignon and he's taking Gaston with him. Gaston is staying with him at the guesthouse until they leave."

"Why would he want Gaston?"

"The marquis hasn't seen him in a while. Perhaps he doesn't know his son is an idiot."

We wanted to go right out and see the procession, but Arlo wouldn't let us. "Full choirs at all Masses today," he said, "and extra rehearsals, too, for a special Mass at daybreak to see them off."

"Leave it to Gaston to ruin another day," grumbled Micah, then he pulled me aside. "How fast can you make some more amulets? We could sell a lot of them to that crowd out there."

All it took was careful planning, a few untruths to the right people, and fast work. We were helped by the general confusion caused by the pilgrims.

"We'll give them away free to children," Micah said. "Everyone else will have to pay."

We left it to each pilgrim to decide what our amulet was worth. Many of them already wore religious symbols, but they were happy to add our magic piece to their collection. They had money, too, and paid us with coin.

"Is there Plague in Avignon?" I asked one old man.

"There is Plague everywhere, but we will not get it. God will spare those who are on a holy mission such as ours," he answered.

"Well, just in case he doesn't, you'd better buy one of these magic amulets," Micah said. We smiled at the old man as he handed over his coin.

By the end of the day, we had a small fortune. We tied it in a bit of cloth, and hid it in our secret hiding place in the crypt. So far, the Plague had been good to us.

The next morning, after early Mass, Gaston said goodbye to the choirboys.

"No more Latin class for me," he bragged. "My father says it's time I began to learn from the world. After all, I'm going to be a very important man in a few years." He had changed out of his choir school robe and was wearing a fine new tunic and surcoat his father had brought him.

"I'll get all new things when I get home from pilgrimage," he said, as he handed out his belongings. He gave his chess set to Arlo and his football to Oswin. To Micah, he gave his old tunic and leggings.

"This is as close as *you'll* ever get to new clothes," he swaggered. Micah did not punch him in the nose—instead, he thanked Gaston.

Out on the road, Gaston took his place beside his father at the head of the procession. We joined the monks in singing a Te Deum as the procession gathered itself up and moved away.

Gaston didn't look so tough anymore. Beside his father, he looked small and, I thought, a little afraid. But I kept that thought to myself.

CHAPTER ELEVEN

We had plenty of warning. We knew the Plague was coming, and we should have been prepared. But was Noah truly prepared for the flood? He might have been told it would happen, and he did as he was told to get ready for it, but I'm certain he was also surprised to see the waters actually rising.

Until you see the earth being flooded, you can't possibly imagine what it means.

Until you see the Plague take a city by its throat, you can't possibly understand what it is all about, and what we went through.

When Brother Marc gets a disturbing picture in his head, he paints the image with his pigments and brush. It is not so scary when it is flat on canvas or parchment, and, he tells me, this will sometimes take the picture out of his dreams. Perhaps as I write about the terrifying sights that I have seen, they will leave my head and stay on the paper, and not trouble me any more. I hope that it will not also tame my good memories of that time, for I have many.

As I have said, we did not expect what came to pass. Before we could understand what we were facing, it was upon us, snarling and snapping, and we could do little to escape its jaws.

A few days after Gaston left the abbey to go on pilgrimage with his father, the choirmaster greeted us with an announcement.

"In this time of Pestilence, His Holiness Pope Clement has ordered those of us in the religious life to go out among the people in devout processions. This is a solemn task we have, boys, a task given to us by the Holy Father himself. I know you will all do your best."

"Will the Bishop be joining us?" Arlo asked.

"The Bishop has retired to his estate in the countryside, to wait out the Pestilence," the choirmaster replied. "He will send out his prayers from there. And now, I want to teach you the new litany we will be singing on our processions."

The litany was a difficult one, but we worked hard, and after a few days of rehearsal, we were ready. Meanwhile, the tailor shop and Brother Marc and his painters made special banners the monks would carry.

"Who is that?" I asked Brother Marc, pointing to the faces on the banners.

"That's St. Benedict, and that," he pointed to another banner, "is the Virgin Mary."

"How do you know what they looked like?"

"This is the way they look in my imagination."

"In my imagination, St. Benedict had a smaller nose."

Brother Marc laughed and was about to reply when the Prior barked at us to get in line.

Micah was crucifer, and I was bellringer, so we had to be at the front of the procession. That morning, the Prior had come to talk to us in the schoolhouse.

"You have heard Brother Sebastien say the Pestilence is caused by an alignment of the planets. Brother Sebastien is a wise man but in this case, he is wrong. The Pestilence is caused by evil, disobedient children!" He stared right at Micah and me.

After the Prior had gone, Micah said to me, "First they say it's the stars, then they say it's the air, now they say the Plague is caused by bad children. I wish they would make up their minds."

"Do you think he's right?" Rafe asked.

"Don't be foolish. The Prior is never right."

"He's just a sour old pickle," Bayard added, and we could all agree on that.

The procession began. The street was muddy from the recent rain. In spots, our feet made sucking sounds each time we lifted them from the mud. We had to move around a cart that was stuck in the middle of the street. The carter pulled and pleaded with his ox to yank the cart free.

I was expecting to see the Paris I had seen before, with Micah. I knew the fair was over, but I thought the city would still be a place of wonder and adventure.

We had been so sheltered at the abbey, walking into Paris was like walking into a bad dream. The city had changed. The Plague had changed it, in just a few short weeks.

"Why are there so many fires?" I asked Brother Kenneth, who walked beside me, when the Prior's attention was elsewhere. The air was thick with smoke, in which I could smell camphor, sage, and orange.

"The smoke is said to clear the air of Plague," Brother Kenneth replied, then went back to chanting.

I saw a home being shut up. "Plague inside! Keep away!" the carpenter said, as he nailed boards across the door. I glimpsed the terrified faces of a family at the window, getting a last breath of fresh air before they were pushed back inside, and the shutters fastened. Their cries were drowned out by the other noises on the street.

"Eat fresh figs!" the fig seller cried. "Figs will protect you from the Plague."

"Eat filberts!" the filbert merchant called out. "The Pestilence will not come to people who eat filberts!"

"We should have brought some Abracadabra amulets to sell," Micah said to me, behind the Prior's back. "We could have made a fortune."

People wandered about looking shocked and lost.

"My family is dead, my family is dead," one old woman mumbled, as she walked by, not seeing our procession or anything else.

A small group of lepers, their ravaged faces covered by rags, held out their long-poled begging bowls.

"Lepers!" a man yelled. "Filthy lepers! They have brought the Plague to our city!" Other men soon joined him, hurling accusations at the lepers, who cowered against the wall of a shop. One of the men picked up a rock and tossed it at the lepers, and others followed his example. A crowd soon gathered. I couldn't see the lepers any more—the crowd was too thick—but I could hear their screams.

"We should do something," I heard Micah say.

"We *are* doing something," the Prior said. "Keep your mind on the psalm."

We moved further into the city. I heard a strange sound coming from behind us. Micah and I looked at each other, puzzled, the turned around and looked behind us.

Ordinary people were following the procession. They came out of houses and off of street corners, and walked along behind us. The strange sound we heard was wailing.

"Why are they wailing?" Hugh, directly behind us, asked.

"I don't know," Micah answered. "Your singing isn't *that* bad."

A Company of Fools

Hugh swatted out at Micah, but was held back by Brother Bart before the Prior could catch on to their misbehavior.

Some parts of Paris looked normal. Shops were open. We saw a goat being slaughtered in the street, a blacksmith pounding at his anvil, and peddlers selling fruit, bread, and cheese off their wagons.

We also saw carts with bodies. In those early days, the carts were covered by a cloth, with only two or three pairs of feet sticking out the end. Mourners followed, weeping. Later, but not much later, there would be too many bodies to worry about hiding the sight of death from the living, and too much death for people to mourn.

We were not far from the square where we were to hold the service when a man stepped out in front of us.

He screamed in agony, and a horrible stench rose from his body. I saw huge black swellings under his arms. He writhed and did a crazy sort of a dance, as if trying to get away from the torment of his body. With one final shriek, he went suddenly rigid, then collapsed in a heap.

Right in front of my horrified eyes, the man died.

CHAPTER TWELVE

✦✦✦

The first Plague victims were shocking. The boils, the dark blotches on their skin, the strange dance they did were terrible to see, but worse was the panic in their eyes and faces.

We didn't see the victims every time we went out on procession, at least not in the beginning. I suppose people preferred privacy when they were dying, and remained in their homes.

At first, we tried to spot them the way people try to spot the first robin in the spring. We choirboys would nudge each other and point when we saw a man on a rooftop doing the strange dance of agony, or a corpse on the street, not yet gathered by the body removers. But when, like the robins, these sights become more regular, we ceased to mark them until they came upon us. Then, walking through Paris was like playing a real-life game of Ghost Jump. We never knew when one of the dying would appear before us, screaming in pain, or eerily silent.

We almost became used to the calls of the body

removers, bells tinkling at their ankles, who pushed handcarts yelling, "Bring out your dead!" We almost became used to seeing the fumigators, dressed in white with red crosses on their necks, who went into homes where all had died, and burned all that could be burned.

We almost became used to it. I find that scary now, to think that we can become used to the suffering of others. Almost. I shall cling to that "almost."

The Plague continued, and so did our processions. All through the autumn of 1348, we went out into the world beyond the walls, in order to...well, I am not certain what we were doing, other than obeying the Pope, which, if you're a monk or a priest or a choirboy, is enough reason to do something.

Unless you're a choirboy named Micah.

"We're bringing people comfort," Arlo insisted.

"No, we're not," Micah insisted right back. "Don't you hear all that wailing from the people who follow us around?"

"People like to wail."

"Nonsense," Micah said. "People like to laugh. And they like to hear me sing, which they can't do as long as all those loud-mouthed monks are chanting and making people wail. Why don't you just admit you don't know why we're doing this any more than I do?"

But Arlo, the brightest boy in school and destined

for the great university of Paris—assuming the world did not come to an end before he had a chance to enrol—would not admit that there was something he did not understand. Or maybe he did not like to admit that Micah, who could not even read, might be right about something.

"The holy processions will end the Plague," Arlo stated, then left the room, so there could be no further argument.

Not all of our processions were grand ones through Paris. Sometimes we went into the little settlements that surround the abbey, and gave services in the village churches. They were not as grand as the cathedral, and our voices did not soar the same way, but they were cozy, and I liked them.

Micah liked them, too. "People should be able to see me when I sing to them," he said. "They should be able to see where the sound they're hearing is coming from."

"Yeah—otherwise they'll think a cow is dying in the choir stall," Bayard replied.

I'd given up trying to explain to Micah that he was singing for the glory of God, not himself. He couldn't understand that, and the more I tried to explain it to him, the less sense it made to me.

"You are supposed to be watching me, Micah," the choirmaster often said, after a visit to one of the small churches, but Micah could not resist looking at people's faces as he sang. I suppose he suffered from the sin of pride, but he had good reason.

One day, we had a different sort of procession. This one was in Paris again.

"Bring out your fanciness!" the Prior called out to the crowd. "Bring out your baubles, your finery, and your pointed shoes, whose very points call down God's wrath upon us!"

The Prior was so worked up, he was actually spitting his words. I was crucifer this time, and I took a step backward to escape the shower. I bumped into Brother Bart, who looked down at me and winked.

Slowly at first, then more and more, people in the crowd came forward with their fancy clothes. They put them on the ground in front of the Prior.

"Pile them up high! Pile up all the things that take your mind off God! Pile up all the items of pride and pretension that have made God angry with you and brought this terrible Pestilence upon your head!"

"At least children are no longer to blame!" Micah leaned over and whispered to me. I started to laugh. The cross I was carrying began to sway, so I had to stop laughing and pay attention.

"Hey, Prior, are you putting *your* gown on the pile?" someone in the crowd called out. The Prior looked ferocious.

The pile of fancy things grew in front of us. Things people had worked for, or inherited, or stolen, things they had been proud to own or had hoarded in secret, were tossed onto the pile as if they were so much rubbish.

Not everyone was willing. A wealthy man came forward, his arms full of colorful women's garments. His wife came running out after him, and tried to take her clothes out of his arms. A tug o' war ensued. The husband and wife cursed each other, forgetting they were in the presence of churchmen. The crowd began to laugh.

With one very loud curse, the man yanked the dresses out of his wife's hands and threw them on the pile. He held his hands over his head, a champion, and bowed to the applauding crowd.

The wife lunged at her husband and grabbed hold of his fine, fur-trimmed cloak. She had it off him before he had a chance to react. The crowd roared their approval.

"This will make a fine addition to the priest's pile!" she yelled. "You strutting peacock!"

The husband turned and grabbed at his cloak, but the stern voice of the Prior stopped him.

"Think not of these things which fill you with conceit!" he boomed. "The fashion of this world passes away. Vanity of vanities, all is vanity!"

After that, the husband had no choice but to walk away, cloakless. We choirboys laughed with the crowd.

"Silence!" roared the Prior. "We will now light the bonfire of the vanities. We will burn all these symbols of human pride and error. With these flames, we will please God, and he will take the Pestilence away!"

I had hoped to be able to light the fire, but the Prior gave himself that fun. The choirmaster raised his hand, which meant we had to look at him instead of the fire. We sang a harsh Dies Irae while the flames grew up into the Paris sky.

Nothing changed. There was no great thunder-clap from heaven as God accepted this sacrifice. None of the sick people around us got better. The Plague took care of the sin of vanity, anyway. On procession one day, I saw a gravedigger wearing a richly embroidered tunic over his usual rags, stolen from the body of someone he'd buried. It was too long for him, and dragged in the dirt. On the way back to the abbey, I saw the same gravedigger. He was dead on the ground.

Late in November, our procession was returning to the abbey. We passed through the gatehouse to the inner yard, when one of the junior monks collapsed, crying out in pain. In a flash, he was carried to the infirmary.

"Our cat is gone," Brother Sebastien told me later that night, as we walked the cloisters together after vespers. "Medicina took one look at the poor, stricken novice, let out a screech, and bounded away through a window. I should not tell you this, Henri, but I fear that is a bad sign."

All night long, the monks kept a vigil in the chapel. Micah and I took our blankets to the balcony, and spent the dark hours there, above the monks, dozing and waking, and watching them pray. Brother Bart came to the schoolhouse at midday to tell us the news.

"Novice Brother Bastien is dead," he said. He sat down at the refectory table with us. He had been up praying all night, and looked very tired.

"I guess God wasn't listening," Micah said.

Brother Bart put his hand over Micah's to silence him.

"There's more," Brother Bart said. "You are all to stay away from the infirmary." He looked especially at me. My panic must have shown on my face, because he said, quickly, "Brother Sebastien is well, but three other Brothers have taken ill."

The Plague had arrived at St. Luc's.

The moment it did, Brother Bart's rosebush burst into bloom, even though the season for roses was long past. It bloomed all that winter, and kept blooming, as long as the Plague was in the abbey.

CHAPTER THIRTEEN

I expect it will be a choirboy who finds and reads this chronicle, and if you are that choirboy, you will be shocked at the following injustice—as we all were, when Arlo brought us the news.

We were sitting around the refectory table, having our supper of cheese, bread and ale, when Arlo returned from meeting with the Prior. He tried to pour himself a mug of ale, but his hands shook so much from anger that he had to put the jug back on the table.

"The Prior is..." Arlo gritted his teeth as he searched for the right phrase. "Not a godly man."

"What did he want to see you about?" Joris asked.

"I didn't think such a thing was possible. I didn't know that priors had that much power," Arlo said, pacing around the table.

"What did he do?" Oswin asked.

"He canceled St. Nicholas Day!"

We were all stunned.

"He didn't actually cancel it," Arlo amended.

"He just forbade us to celebrate it."

"But that's *our* day!" Hugh said. "St. Nicholas belongs to the choirboys, not to a moldy old prior."

"He did say we could have supper in the main refectory with the monks if we promised to be quiet. But no feast, no celebration, and no Boy Bishop."

Dear Reader, if you are who I think you are, you know what a crime against choirboys this was, and what an uproar rang out in the schoolhouse. Loudest of all was Micah, who didn't really know what he was angry about, except that someone he didn't like was taking something away from him.

"But *I'm* Boy Bishop!" Micah yelled. "I won it in a bet!"

"Next year," Arlo said.

"By next year, we could all be dead of the Plague. It has to be this year."

"How could we be dead of the Plague if we're wearing these amulets you sold us?" Bayard asked.

Micah waved the question away. "The Prior isn't going to tell *me* what to do."

"Or me," declared Oswin. Everyone else, even Arlo and I, agreed with Micah.

Brother Thomas, the housemaster, discreetly removed himself from the schoolhouse. He had a good nose for knowing when we needed him around, and when we needed him to disappear.

"We've got to make plans," Micah said.

"Do you even know who St. Nicholas was?" Arlo asked him.

"What? No. Does it matter?"

"If we're going to go against the Prior and celebrate St. Nicholas Day behind his back, wouldn't you like to know what it is?"

Micah shrugged and grinned in that way he had when he didn't care that someone was trying to insult him. "So tell me."

Oswin spoke up. "A thousand years ago, there was a horrible butcher who had three small sons. He chopped them up and put their body parts in a barrel of vinegar, and was going to sell them as meat to his customers. St. Nicholas came by, and with a wave of his hand, made the boys whole again and brought them back to life."

"Oh, Oswin, that's just a legend," Arlo said. "This is what really happened. A man was going to sell his three daughters into slavery because he couldn't afford to keep them. St. Nicholas threw three bags of money into the house, and saved the girls."

"He's also the patron saint of sailors," I said. "He guides them to safety when they're in a storm."

"And he rescues people from prison," Arlo added.

That was enough information for Micah. "How do we celebrate?"

"We have a great big feast, and the Boy Bishop gets dressed up and acts like a bishop for a day," I said.

"We can do almost anything we want to and we won't get into trouble," Oswin said. "It's wonderful."

"Why doesn't the Prior want us to celebrate this year?" I asked.

"He said it would be unseemly for us to be celebrating when people are dying," Arlo replied.

"People are always dying," Micah said. "The Prior would like us to spend our whole lives weeping." He jumped up on the table, knocking over Fabien's mug of ale, which Felix lapped up as it dripped to the floor. Then Micah did some dance steps on the tabletop while he chanted, "I want to be happy, happy, happy, happy!"

"Come on up here, fellows," he challenged. "Let's show the sour old pickle just what we think of him." He began singing the song about the drunken bishop, the song he sang when he first came to the abbey. By the end of the first verse, we were all dancing on the tabletop. Even Arlo. Even me.

I've danced on many tabletops since that day. I hope to dance on many more. Even when I'm an old, old monk of thirty, I'll still haul myself up on a table and do a few feeble steps before dropping from exhaustion. It makes you feel good, to be up high and hearing the rhythm of your feet on the wood. Why not try it now, dear reader? Just don't step on the Chronicle.

That was the best St. Nicholas Day I've ever had.

I was a part of things. I didn't hang back and watch the other boys celebrate, pretending to be more interested in reading my book. I was right there with the others, laughing and running through the abbey and stuffing myself with all the glorious food a few friendly monks smuggled into the schoolhouse.

We dressed Micah up like a bishop. (Don't ask me how we got the vestments out of Brother Sacristan's locked cupboards, as I am sworn to secrecy.) We carried him on a chair through the cathedral. Micah wanted us to do it while services were on, but Arlo wouldn't let us. It was still fun, even if no one saw us but a few villagers come to pray for deliverance from the Plague.

In between meals, we played an extended game of Ghost Jump. At night, we all went up into the bell tower and howled at the world, as snow began to fall.

It was a perfect day. We were lucky to have had it. For shortly after that, everything began to change.

Pope Clement put an end to the processions.

"It's not healthy to bring large crowds of people together when there is Pestilence," Brother Sebastien said, on one of our walks around the cloisters. "His Holiness has made a wise decision."

"First he says processions are good, then he says they're bad," was Micah's reaction. "The Pope doesn't know what he's doing." And just between you and me, Reader, I found myself agreeing with him.

When the processions ended, the only contact we had with the outside world was at funerals. The Plague had taken away many a parish priest, so the Abbot and other senior monks left the abbey to perform these services, accompanied by Micah and me. Most of the boys had families who paid good money to keep them safe, and the Abbot had decreed they should remain within abbey walls. Only Micah and I had no one, so we spent much of our time going from grave to grave, singing the Requiem so many times it lost all meaning.

On a chilly day at the end of January, Micah and I and some of the brothers were gathered with the Abbot on a scratchy bit of wasteland outside the Paris walls. We stood at the edge of a great hole, and in that hole were the bodies of men, women, and children, all taken by that great devil, Pestilence. The good were there along with the bad, the rich along with the poor, the loved along with the lonely. They were all together, for there weren't enough gravediggers left to dig them each their own grave.

The air was thick with smoke, from the incense burning in the censer that I swung, and from the bonfires purifying the air. The smoke was not enough, not nearly enough, to take away the stench of death.

I leaned forward a bit, to peer down into the pit, and immediately wished I hadn't. The bodies were tossed in any which way. They were black and bloody, and many had their eyes open, as if death had grabbed them by surprise when they were in the middle of doing something else. The stench was overwhelming.

My mind searched wildly for a distraction, and landed on the St. Nicholas Day celebration, held a few weeks ago. How Micah had strutted around the cathedral, as if he were the real Bishop! How we had laughed! And the feast! Pork pies, cheese, roasted goose....

Thoughts of food mixed with the stink of death, and I had to quickly step out of the service to vomit. One of the monks handed me a cloth to wipe my mouth. There was no shame. I was not the first one to throw up at a funeral.

> Dance, little dog, said the Raven to the Cur,
> Dance on your toes and feel the wind in your fur,
> Dance and spin 'til the bright day is done,
> And me and my lady will join in the fun.

At first I thought I was going mad. How could I be hearing a happy song at a funeral? Then I realized Micah was singing.

There was a puppy nearby, chasing its tail and hopping around happily. Micah's song gave it music to dance to. Small children who had been watching the funeral with forlorn little faces started laughing. Grown men and women laughed, too.

Brother Bart was the first monk to laugh, and he started us all laughing. Not even the Abbot could keep a solemn face. The little dog kept dancing to Micah's tune.

Micah launched into another song, and when the puppy dashed off to explore somewhere else, Micah started dancing, too. He grabbed me and twirled me, and I joined him in song. People clapped their hands, keeping time.

We sang three songs together before I felt the Abbot's gentle hand on my shoulder.

"Very nice, boys," he said. "Now let us send the unfortunate ones off into Heaven with a joyful In Paradisum, so that they may arrive in the next world with a smile on their faces."

Micah and I stood together beside the pit of death and sang an In Paradisum so bright and clear, I am sure it reached God's gates and pushed them open.

I felt useful. I felt that I had given the dead ones a gift. It made me joyful.

CHAPTER FOURTEEN

Micah later claimed it was all his idea. He forgot I was with him in the scriptorium when Brother Bart came in to talk to Brother Marc.

We were watching Brother Marc paint a picture of grinning skeletons dancing with townspeople. Death danced across the page, arm in arm with beautiful women, with farmers and with clergy.

"Hello, Brother Marc," said Brother Bart, as he entered the scriptorium, puffing a little from the walk up the winding staircase. "Hello, boys. I'm glad you are here as well. Father Abbot and I have been discussing your performance at the graveside the other day."

"I suppose we are in trouble," Micah said, although he did not sound concerned.

"Not at all. The Abbot thinks you may be able to help us with a special mission."

"What sort of mission?"

"Making people happy. This is not an official mission, you understand," he said to Brother Marc. "It hasn't been officially sanctioned. Father Abbot merely said that if a few monks—and boys—want to take on the task of bringing some relief to people's spirits, he would not interfere."

Brother Marc set aside his drawing of the dance of death. "Did Father Abbot suggest how we should accomplish this?"

"Father Abbot left that to our own good judgment. 'Make a joyful noise unto the Lord,' he said. He believes that God must be tired of lamentations, and the sound of laughter might please him."

Micah and I looked from one monk to the other, then watched Brother Marc take up a piece of charcoal and sketch out an idea.

"We will still be monks," Brother Marc said, "but we will do things not expected of us, and that will make people laugh."

"Like two choirboys dancing at a funeral," I said.

"Or like the bishop being played by the baddest boy in the abbey," Micah added.

"Yes, yes," said Brother Bart, "and the monks can sing songs of humor and irreverence, and dance around in a most unseemly manner."

Brother Marc's charcoal flew across the paper. "What will we call this?" he asked.

"The Idiots of St. Luc's," Brother Bart suggested. "Or the Order of Mad Monks?"

"Henri and I aren't monks," Micah said. "I think we should call ourselves Two Choirboys and their

Foolish Company."

"How about the Company of Fools?" I suggested. After some discussion, that is what we decided to call ourselves. Now it is a matter of historical record that the idea for the name was mine. That is one advantage of being chronicler.

Brother Kenneth joined immediately. So did Brother Marc, Brother Joel, Brother Jude the cellarer, and Brother Jerome, who brewed the abbey's ale.

Brother Marc engaged the labors of monks in the tailor shop for the making of costumes. Brother Jude was transformed into a donkey, Brother Kenneth into a sheep, and Brother Jerome into a rooster. Brother Joel carved dozens of tiny wooden toys for us to hand out to children we saw.

Micah was Boy Bishop again. The sacristan, backed up by the Abbot, absolutely refused to let us use the Bishop's real vestments. "They're too big for me anyway," Micah said. The tailors made up other robes for him.

"What would you like to be?" Brother Marc asked me. I had no idea.

"Why don't you be a jester, the sort of fellow who makes kings and queens laugh?"

I liked that idea. He designed for me a costume of motley, many colors. I carried a little drum, and wore a cap with ribbons flowing from it. I looked as grand as Micah.

"Don't you wish you were us?" We boasted to the other boys in the schoolhouse. We were showing off our costumes. They looked at us with envy, especially since we had been let off singing at ordinary services to do the Company of Fools. I let Rafe beat my drum for a little while.

"I'd much rather stay here," Garwood lied. "It won't matter if you die, but if I die, who will take over my father's land? Go wander among the Pestilence if you want to, but I'm much too important."

Micah and I treated Garwood with the disdain he deserved, and went off to practice our dances. The Company rehearsed in the wine cellar, among the giant casks of wine.

Finally, the Company of Fools was ready.

Micah rode into Paris on a small cart pulled by one of the abbey's donkeys. I rode with him as far as the city walls, then got out to walk in front of the monks, beating my drum to get people's attention.

There was a lot of competition. A group of peasants with skeleton bones painted on their tunics danced and sang. "The rich will die along with the poor! Long live the Plague!" Peddlers sold all manner of Plague cures, spells, and amulets, which I thought looked fake compared to our Abracadabra ones. There was a puppet show going on, too. In the show, Death was trying to take away a woman's child. The woman kept hitting Death on the head with a club, but Death kept trying. It was not a funny puppet show, and no one laughed.

A woman passed by us, crying in pain. People pointed at her and laughed.

"Why do you laugh at her misfortune?" I heard Brother Joel ask.

"You can catch the Plague by watching someone else's agony, you know," the man answered, "but if you laugh, you confuse it, and it goes looking for some other miserable wretch to make a home in. Besides, I've lost my wife and three children to the Pestilence. If I start crying, I'll never stop, and the Plague will take me for sure."

"Then we will help you to laugh," Brother Bart said. To the Company of Fools he said, "Let's begin."

Brother Kenneth stepped forward. He had the biggest voice in the abbey. In his former life, he had been a town crier. He took a deep breath and belted out the introduction.

"We are the Company of Fools! Gather round for the Company of Fools!"

People drifted toward us. We sang our opening song, which we had composed one night after vespers. I banged on my drum to keep time. At the end of each chorus the monks made the sign of the cross, but did it wrong, and got tangled up in their gestures.

The crowd laughed! I looked at people's faces. Gone were the lines of worry, the pallor of fear. Life was beginning to dance in their eyes.

Brother Kenneth stepped forward again. "Our bishop is about to sing! Come close and hear the most holy message of our beloved bishop!"

Micah rose and stood grandly in the donkey cart. He sang a song the Company had written about what a wonderful bishop he was—brave (he cowered), sober (he took a drink from a water-filled wine jug), and holy (he tried to cross himself but could not get it right). He sang about the brilliance of his sermons (we pretended to sleep), the loyalty of his congregation (we brayed like sheep), and the prettiness of the nuns who looked after him. He also sang about his great humility. "I am the most humble bishop in all the land!"

Then we all sang and danced. Micah kept taking drinks from the wine jug, acting so drunk he fell out of the donkey cart and into Brother Bart's arms. Brother Bart put him back in upside-down, so that his legs waved wildly where his head should have been.

The more we did, the more people laughed. The more they laughed, the healthier they looked. The only people who looked gloomy were the people selling Plague cures. They weren't making any money!

At the end of the performance, Brother Kenneth boomed out, "Make a joyful noise unto the Lord!" and "Do unto others as you would have them do unto you!"

It felt good to be laughing and making people laugh. I felt powerful, as though, perhaps, we could defeat the Plague after all.

Every few days the Company of Fools went out. We performed wherever there were people. We sang our silly songs and danced in our mad, colorful costumes. Sometimes my mind would stand as if apart from the rest of me, and would watch me dancing and singing and making a fool of myself in front of strangers. I hardly recognized myself. Had I really been that shy boy who buried himself in books and never laughed out loud?

Now that I am back again among my beloved volumes, I can hardly believe that I wore my jester costume of many colors and made myself ridiculous, and enjoyed myself while I was doing it. For we did have fun. The sights we saw were terrible; the people who came to us were suffering greatly; and, I suppose, we put ourselves in danger every time we went out into the Plague's domain.

Yet I will not deny it. We had fun. We had fun while we were making up songs; we had fun while we were performing; and we had fun when we returned to the abbey, to eat supper in the wine cellar, our laughter bouncing off the wine casks.

There will never be another time in my life like it. I hold the memories close to me, as a precious, precious gift.

CHAPTER FIFTEEN

On procession in the early days of the Plague, whenever we went through a village, I watched for families. I craned my neck to try to see inside their houses. I tried to imagine what it is like to sleep in a room with a family, instead of in a dormitory with twelve other choirboys. I wondered what mealtimes were like, and what it would be like to be around a mother and a father every day.

I particularly watched the women.

My early life was spent with nuns, and we see women sometimes in the almshouse, but I confess that girls and women are still very mysterious to me. Since my life might well be spent behind these walls, they will likely remain a mystery.

So, yesterday I asked Brother Bart to tell me everything he knew about women. He told me they are complex creatures of great beauty and wonder, but even with his vast experience, he still found them to be a mystery.

"Do you miss them?" I asked.

A wistful sort of expression came over his face, more wistful than usual, I mean, and he said, simply, "Yes."

Perhaps by the time this chronicle is discovered, the mystery of women will be solved, although I fear it will be too late for me to gain any wisdom from it.

This is not what I wanted to write about today, but it is pleasanter to think about women than it is to remember the events I must now relate, events which changed all our lives, particularly Micah's. Though there is reason for wandering onto the subject of women: the memory I am thinking of now has nuns in it, as well as a little girl, which are both a type of woman, are they not?

The Company of Fools was performing in the Hotel Dieu, the great hospital in Paris. I had not known such a place existed. If I had lived in the world, perhaps my frail health would have had me spending as much time there as I spent in Brother Sebastien's infirmary. The thought fills me with gratitude for being a choirboy.

"This is a horrible place," I heard Micah say to Brother Bart. "Let's get out of here." I felt the same, and moved closer to Brother Bart for protection.

"These are people in torment," Brother Bart replied. "They need us. Look at me when you are singing, and you will be all right."

It was easier to look at Brother Bart than at the

patients, crammed three or four into a bed. The sounds and smells that came from them were truly horrible. Never before had we been surrounded so intensely by Plague victims.

"I don't want to do this," Micah insisted. "I want to go."

"Very well," Brother Bart said. "We will go."

A few moments earlier, when we had just arrived, the Mother Superior had told us they lost hundreds of patients every day. The nuns of her convent were the nurses at the hospital. "The sisters do the best they can," Mother Superior had said, "but it is not much beyond giving the sick a bit of comfort, and letting them know they are not alone when they die. Most have been abandoned by their families. We are all they have."

I thought of these words as we stood in the ward, considering. I would not like to be in one of those beds, with no one to comfort me. All around were nuns, wiping brows, holding hands, and giving drinks of tea, but there were many more patients than there were nuns.

I know what it is like to be ill. I know how lonely it is to be near death. As I stood among the whimpers and wails and stench and fear, I heard myself say, "No. We'll stay."

By this time, Micah was almost out the door of the ward. He turned back.

"I'll do your part," I said to him. "It will be all right. I know how it goes."

Micah, looking very huffy, put the bishop's miter back on his head and rejoined the Company. "What are we waiting for?" he snarled.

Brother Bart winked at me, then nodded for Brother Kenneth to begin.

"We are the Company of Fools," Brother Kenneth announced loudly, but not as loudly as he did in the marketplace. "We know you are ill, and we will try in our small way to make you feel better."

We began to sing our songs. I saw some faces change from masks of agony to smiles. Some of the patients even laughed.

The nuns laughed, too, and for a little while, they did not look so tired.

We went from ward to ward. I don't know how many times we performed our act. We just kept singing.

We finished our round of songs and were about to move on to another ward when I realized Micah was on the other side of the room.

"Go tell Micah we're moving on," Brother Bart said.

Just then, Micah began to sing. It was a song I had not heard him sing before, sweet and clear, rising above the stinking ward like birdsong. I went over and stood beside him, by the bed of a young girl, younger than Rafe. She had a bed to herself, and looked so tiny and delicate there.

The bed was draped differently from the other hospital beds, with fine linens and velvet covers. A man sat on a chair by the bed. He was dressed in rich clothes, and sat with his head in his hands, bowed over by grief.

As Micah finished the song, the man raised his head, and looked at him.

"Your voice has touched me," he said. "It has brought me the first moments of peace I have had in days." He reached into the pouch at his belt. "Take this," he said, handing Micah a coin. "Sing some more. Perhaps your voice can bring peace to my little Azura as well."

My eyes widened. The coin the man was holding out was gold. Micah raised his hand to receive it. He was beaten to it by Brother Bart, who closed the man's fingers around his offering.

"We are from the Abbey of St. Luc," Brother Bart said. "No payment is necessary."

Now it was Micah's turn to widen his eyes, as he stared in disbelief at Brother Bart.

"Go ahead, Micah," Brother Bart said, "Sing some more."

Micah swallowed hard as he watched the coin disappear into the rich man's purse. He looked like he was going to refuse to sing, then his eyes fell again on the little girl on the bed. He opened his mouth, and sang.

When he was done, the man thanked us, and we left. And that would have been the end of the matter, except that the rich man showed up at the abbey a week later.

Micah and I were doing our usual spying on Chapter House discussions. When we got there, the rich man from the hospital, whose name turned out to be Lord Morley, was with the monks, talking, as we inched open the door from the catacombs.

"What's he doing here?" Micah whispered.

I shook my head. Why would I know?

"We did everything we could to protect her from the Plague," Lord Morley was saying. "We left the city and barricaded ourselves in at our country estate, just me, my wife, our daughter Azura, our closest friends, and our most trusted servants. We had the choicest food, the finest wine, and the lightest entertainment to keep us laughing. I have heard that the Plague comes more quickly to those who are morose."

Out in the catacombs, I wondered if that were true. I decided to ask Brother Sebastien the next time we walked in the cloisters.

"But still the Plague found us," Lord Morley went on. "My little daughter collapsed at a banquet, the telltale swellings under her arm. I used my fastest horses to bring her to the hospital in Paris, whose reputation is renowned. For three days I sat by her chair, watching her slip away from me.

"Then a sound came to my ears. It was sweet and clear, like it belonged to a bird from heaven. It gave me a glimpse of the beauty of the world, in the midst of stench and despair of this horrible Pestilence. It brought me out from my sorrow for a brief moment.

"Good monks, that sound came from a boy attached to this abbey. He wore the robes of a bishop, and he stood by my daughter's bed and sang to her, one gentle song after another, until he was led away by one of the monks with him.

"I slipped into a doze, then. I dreamed of my daughter. In the dream Azura was calling to me. 'Papa . . . Papa . . . I'm thirsty!'

"Then I realized it was not a dream! I became fully awake, to see my child looking at me with clear eyes, asking for water.

"I leapt off my chair. 'Water! Water! We need water!' I was so happy, I was weeping like an infant. One of the good nuns brought water. Azura drank, then fell back again, into a sleep that was only sleep. Soon she was well again."

Beside me, in the passageway, Micah was barely breathing. I think he knew what Lord Morley was about to say next.

Lord Morley stood up. "That boy cured my child," he said. "It is the greatest miracle since the raising of Lazarus. Good brothers, I believe that boy has been sent to us from God to rid the world of this terrible Plague. He brought my daughter back from the dead. I believe he can also bring life to the rest of the world."

The monks reacted to this pronouncement with stunned silence. I looked at Micah. He was grinning.

The Abbot was the first to speak. "Is there something you wish us to do?"

"Yes, Father Abbot, there is. I wish you to give me permission to spread the news of this miracle, so that the boy's voice might reach all the people it can. I ask this so that I might pay for the life of my daughter by saving the lives of others."

I moved around a little so that I could see the Prior. His face was turning purple, but I knew he would not say anything that might contradict the Abbot, not in front of the guest.

The Abbot spoke again. "What you propose could cause considerable disruption to an abbey already under great strain from the Pestilence."

"I do not mean to add to your burdens," said Lord Morley. "Perhaps you would permit me to ease your cares somewhat. I own a large estate in the province neighboring this one. It has good land, sturdy buildings, and peasants who know how to work. I will make your order a gift of this estate and its servants, in return for this great favor I ask of you."

"Good Lord Morley, your request is a small one," said Father Abbot. "We will see what we can do. Please make yourself comfortable in my private quarters. I will join you there directly, and share with you some of the abbey's very fine wine."

Lord Morley bowed, and left the chapter house. As soon as the door closed behind him, Father Prior exploded.

"Blasphemy!"

"No, Father Prior, it is not blasphemy," Father Abbot said, calmly. "It is merely the opinion of a man who came very close to losing what he values most, and wants to give thanks for God's mercy."

"But to give that boy—*that boy*—any notion of elevated status! He is already a pox upon this cathedral! This must not happen!"

"Father Abbot, I agree with Father Prior," Brother Bart said. I felt Micah jump a little with surprise. "We do not share the same opinion of Micah's character, but I do think this would be a mistake."

"Imagine saying that brat was sent by God to save us all," sputtered the Prior. "I still say it's blasphemy."

"Father Prior, in ordinary times, we might have been able to indulge ourselves with a blasphemy trial, but these are not ordinary times. Of course Micah did not cure that girl. It was God's will that cured her. If he wishes to thank God for that, we will accept the man's gift on that basis."

The Abbot stood up. "Brother Bartholemew, you will continue entertaining in the streets with this Company of yours. We, ourselves, will do nothing to promote the notion of Micah as a balm for Plague sufferers, but if the word is spread by Lord Morley or his confederates, you will not dispute it. You will use it to bring people greater comfort."

The Abbot began to leave the chapter house.

"Father Abbot," Brother Bart called after him, "I beg you, please, do not do this. I fear it will be harmful to the boy."

Father Abbot stopped. "Brother Bartholemew, it will be up to you to see the boy is not harmed. He is, after all, your responsibility. When we are facing what could be the end of the world, the well-being of one small boy is not very important. And who knows? Perhaps Lord Morley is right. You brought Micah to us because you thought he was special. This will give him a chance to prove you right. God works in mysterious ways, you know."

The Abbot left the chapter house, followed by the rest of the brothers. Brother Bart waited until they had all left. Then he looked directly at the secret door where Micah and I were hiding. Slowly and sadly, he shook his head, then went out into the cloisters.

CHAPTER SIXTEEN

I wish I could say that Micah didn't change. I wish I could record here that he was not touched by the hysteria that followed Lord Morley's appearance before Chapter House, but there is nothing to be gained by wishing the past were different.

I don't blame Micah, though. I could never blame Micah.

We left the secret door in the chapter house that day and went straight up to the bell tower. News as exciting as this required us to be up high. The Feast of the Annunciation was around the corner. The air was still chilly, but it smelled like spring. We inhaled the breeze in great gulps, catching our breath from the dash up to the tower from the catacombs.

"He must be terribly rich," Micah said. It did not surprise me that his first thoughts were of money.

"Did you hear the way he gave all that land to the monks?" I said. "As casual as if he were handing them an old sandal."

"Maybe he'll take us to live on one of his estates,"

Micah said. "We'll be rich, too! I'll marry his daughter and become Lord Micah."

"What will I do?"

"You'll be our friend. Maybe he'll have a daughter for you, too."

The idea of us being married was so silly it started us giggling, even though it is not unusual for marriage to be thought of for boys our age. Oswin already had a bride promised to him, as did Dermot. Neither were bad fellows, but Dermot had smelly feet, and we felt sorry for his future wife.

The Abbot may have nurtured a secret hope that Lord Morley would hand over his land without expecting St. Luc's to keep its part of the bargain, but that was not the case. Lord Morley sent an escort for the Company, two men in scarlet tunics, each carrying a trumpet. They were waiting for us at the gatehouse the next time the Company set out to perform.

"With Lord Morley's compliments, we are to go with you to announce the miraculous powers of the boy called Micah."

"The boy has no such powers," Brother Bart said. "So please do not trouble yourselves."

"We are here under the orders of Lord Morley, and with the blessing of your abbot," one of them replied. Brother Bart could say nothing further against them, then. He was under the vow of Holy Obedience. He said no more to the trumpeters, but led the Company out into the road to Paris.

Micah and I, riding together in the donkey cart, laughed with each other at how alike the two trumpeters were, down to the cut of their hair and the design of their faces. This would be the last time we would joke like this on the Company's business. I wish I had paid more attention, but it seemed too much like an ordinary day.

Brother Bart led the Company to Paris at a good, strong pace. I think he was hoping the men from Lord Morley would lag behind and lose their way, but the trumpeters' legs were as strong as Brother Bart's, and they kept up with the Company.

We stopped in a clearing just inside the city walls. "We'll begin here," Brother Bart said. I got out of the donkey cart and took up my usual position.

"Should we not go to where there are more people?" one of the trumpeters asked.

"This spot will do," was Brother Bart's reply.

"I fear my Lord Morley will be displeased with such a small audience."

Brother Bart looked at the trumpeters, then at the other brothers. He shook his head. "Very well," he said. We moved deeper into the city, where the crowd was larger.

Brother Kenneth stepped forward to boom out his customary greeting to the crowd. He had just taken a deep breath when the trumpeters stepped in front of him and blew loud, strong notes through their horns.

"Gather round!" the trumpeters called out. They spoke in unison, their voices together almost as loud as Brother Kenneth's on its own. "Witness the miracle worker, young Micah of St. Luc's, who did, with the glory of his voice, cure the daughter of our beloved Lord Morley. Gather round, that his voice might cure you as well!"

"That is not why we're here!" Brother Jude said angrily.

"That is why *we're* here," one of the trumpeters replied, then they called to the crowd again. "Come hear the voice of young Micah, wonder child of St. Luc's, and let it cure you of the Plague as it cured Lord Morley's daughter!"

I thought that people would have been tired of Plague cures, but they seemed hungrier than ever. Soon there was a large crowd around us. It was a different type of crowd than we usually had. People weren't coming to us with the look people get when you do something for them that is nice and unexpected, and simply a gift. These faces said something different. I'd seen it before, at the almshouse when we had a large crowd of beggars, and they weren't sure there was enough bread to go around.

"Are you the one? Can you save me from the Plague?" Some of the people in the crowd thought

I was Micah, and they pushed in around me, grabbing at me. "Save me! Save me!" they cried.

Their pleading, desperate faces terrified me. I shrank from them, burying my face in Brother Joel's robe. Brother Joel put me behind him. I peered out at the crowd between him and Brother Marc.

"He's not the one! I am!" Micah stood up in the donkey cart. I looked up at him. He had his hands on his hips, looking much the way he had looked when Brother Bart first brought him to the abbey.

"Brother Kenneth, if you would, please," said Brother Bart.

"Certainly." Brother Kenneth took a deep breath and boomed out his usual Company of Fools introduction. We began our opening song. I glanced up at Micah as I banged my drum. He was sitting back down, arms entwined across his chest, sulking.

"We want to hear the boy!" someone in the crowd shouted. His demand started the others off. "Let the boy sing!" Brother Bart gave Lord Morley's messengers a very un-monk-like glare. They smugly smiled back at him.

There was no point in continuing with the rest of the Company of Fools routine. Brother Bart gave a nod to do Micah's Boy Bishop introduction. Brother Kenneth did, and Micah began singing.

We went through the song with him, the same as usual, but I looked at the brothers and thought they were thinking the same thing that I was, that things were not the same as usual.

Micah finished the bishop song and launched immediately into another solo, even though the next song was supposed to be with the whole company. I looked at the brothers to see what I was supposed to do. They looked as uncertain as I was.

Every time one of Micah's songs ended, the crowd began to chant, "Micah! Micah!" Micah's face shone as he heard them. His body rocked a little in time with the chant. "Micah! Micah!"

In the middle of his fourth solo, I saw Brother Bart whisper to Brother Marc, who took hold of the donkey's reins and led it away so abruptly, Micah dropped into his seat with a clunk. The crowd followed us, still chanting, "Micah! Micah!" Micah turned back in his seat and tried to keep singing, but it was impossible. The jerkiness of the cart over the rough cobblestones kept him from getting a good breath to sing with.

The crowd followed us out of the Paris gates, gathering people as it went. "Micah! Micah!" they kept chanting.

I stayed in tight between Brother Joel and Brother Bart, away from the desperate people. At one point, they crowded in so close around us, I was terrified we would be crushed.

Brother Kenneth took the trumpet out of one of

the escort's hands, climbed up on the cart, and sent a blast of sound out over the crowd.

"Good people, let us pass! Young Micah must return now to St. Luc's to rest. Go back to your homes." He said the part about making a joyful noise and doing unto others, but I doubt anyone paid attention to that. For a moment, I was afraid the crowd was going to disobey him; then it parted, and allowed us to move through. Still, they kept up their chanting: "Micah! Micah!"

They didn't leave us, though. Some may have gone back to their homes, but most followed us all the way to St. Luc's.

"Why did you stop me singing?" Micah demanded of Brother Bart.

"Because you were beginning to believe what was being said of you," Brother Bart answered, walking beside the donkey cart. "You cannot cure the Plague. You have no special powers. You are only a boy."

"How do you know?" Micah challenged. "You don't know anything! Everyone says so. The only thing you're good for is cleaning out the cesspits!"

Brother Bart kept walking. He did not look at Micah, and he did not reply.

CHAPTER SEVENTEEN

Micah was angry at Brother Bart. Brother Bart was angry at Micah, and, I think, at the Abbot and Lord Morley. I was angry at Micah for saying those things to Brother Bart, and told him so. Micah accused me of not believing in him. I didn't know how to reply to that, and Micah became angry with me. It was a strange, angry time, and I did not know how to make things better.

I would have talked about this with Brother Sebastien, but I rarely saw him anymore. The infirmary was forbidden to anyone who did not have the Plague, or who wasn't assisting Brother Sebastien. It's a good thing my fevers had stopped. There was nowhere for me to be ill.

Sometimes I would go to the infirmary and stand outside, looking in the window. Brother Sebastien was always there, on his feet, caring for a brother down with the Plague. He made them teas for pain and to help them sleep, and poultices for the ugly black boils under their arms.

Those who were clearly dying were all grouped together, and kept separated from those who were newly stricken. I remembered what that man in the street had said, about how someone could catch the Plague just by seeing someone else's suffering.

Some monks died quickly. Some suffered for weeks. Occasionally, a monk recovered. He stayed on in the infirmary, helping Brother Sebastien. No one said the monk recovered because of Micah's voice. Micah never went near the infirmary.

Brother Sebastien had his assistants working in shifts, constantly scrubbing every inch of the infirmary with hot water and vinegar. No sooner would a monk finish washing the floor when he would begin washing it all over again. It was necessary. The Plague was a messy disease.

Roses from Brother Bart's rosebush stood in vases beside each bed. Their scent cleared the air of the stink of the Plague. No matter how long the stems stayed in the vases, the flowers never wilted. No matter how many roses were cut from the bush, the bush was always full. Such a miracle made me think that maybe Lord Morley was right. Maybe Micah could cure the Plague.

But if he could, why were so many monks dying? They had all heard him sing. The more I thought about it, the more confused I became.

I would have kept visiting the infirmary window,

just to be near Brother Sebastien, but he spotted me one day, and chased me away. "Get away from this place! It is not safe for you here!"

I knew he was thinking of my health, but I was still hurt. Later, he sent a messenger over to the school-house for me, asking me to meet him at the laboratory.

"I could use your help," he said, and showed me how to mix up the drink he gave to Plague patients, a blend of apple syrup, lemon, rosewater, and peppermint.

"It is a soothing drink," he said, giving me a taste, "but it is not a cure. There is so little we know. Is it better to lance the boils or leave them alone? Why do some patients die quickly, and others linger? Does bleeding them help, or does it make things worse? We know so very little."

"Maybe Micah should come here and sing," I suggested. "He cured that little girl, after all."

Brother Sebastien paused in the stirring of his mixture, looked at me, and said, "Your friend will have great need of you in the time to come."

I laughed. "Micah doesn't need anybody."

Brother Sebastien put his hand on my shoulders and turned me to face him. "It takes courage to be a real friend," he said. "Micah *will* need you. Watch for the moment, and be ready. Do not disappoint him."

I still did not understand him, but he did not explain further, and I was left to ponder his words on my own.

I took on the task of keeping the infirmary supplied with Plague drink. When we ran out of actual lemons, and could not get more because the Plague had interrupted trade, I substituted lemon balm. It made no difference.

Sometimes Brother Sebastien gave me a list of plants to gather and prepare. I took Rafe and Reverdy, the youngest boys, with me to the herb garden. They were pleasant little boys, and in awe of me since I was older, but it wasn't like being with Brother Sebastien, or with Micah.

The people who followed us home from Paris remained on the green outside the abbey walls all night long. They kept up their chant of "Micah! Micah!" until very late, then began it again when dawn broke the next morning.

I sought out Brother Bart after the morning service. "Who are those people? Why don't they go away?"

"They are desperate people, in need of hope," he answered. We were both in the vestry with the other choirboys. He had assisted at Mass and was hanging up his vestments. "In ordinary times, they would be at their usual labors, but..."

"These are not ordinary times," I finished for him. "What are we going to do?"

Brother Bart looked over at where Micah was taking off his surplice. Micah did not look at him. Brother Bart sighed, slowly, and said, "We are going to continue to do the best we can. In the meantime, you have Latin to learn, and I have cesspits to clean."

It was not much of an answer, but I found it comforting. It was reassuring to be back in Latin class, too. Because of the Company of Fools, I had not gone regularly for a while. Virgil was still the same, and Horace, and so were the strings of verbs I had to learn. The world may change, but Latin is the same forever, and cesspits will always need cleaning.

That day, at our midday meal, I was sitting across from Micah as usual, but Micah wasn't talking to me. He was arguing with the others.

"How many people did you save yesterday, Micah?" teased Fabien.

"You just wish you had special powers, like me," Micah replied.

"Do you save boys as well as girls?" jeered Oswin.

"Why don't you go sing in the crypt?" Joris asked. "I would love to see all those dead abbots get up out of their coffins and dance around."

"I don't care if you don't believe in me," Micah declared.

"Look, Micah, here's a dead fly. Sing to it, will you? Make it fly again." Bayard flicked the fly across the table at Micah.

The other boys found this terribly funny. Micah stabbed his pottage with his spoon. "You can all go ahead and die! I'm not singing for any of you!"

"You forget," Oswin said, "we've had to listen to your lousy voice every day in the cathedral for nearly a year. We couldn't catch the Plague now if we wanted to—if you're magic, that is. Plus, we have these!" Oswin waggled his Abracadabra talisman at Micah.

Micah leapt across the table at Oswin and rolled him to the floor. The other boys formed a ring around them, urging Oswin on. I remained at the table. I didn't know what to do. It felt like the old days again, when I was outside of things.

Brother Thomas, our housemaster, came into the schoolhouse, and had Micah and Oswin separated in a moment. They tried to throw insults at each other, but Brother Thomas silenced them.

"You must all be very quiet," he said. "I've come to tell you that our beloved Abbot has just died."

The younger boys began to cry.

"Did he die of Plague?" Arlo asked.

"Yes," said Brother Thomas. "It was the Plague."

CHAPTER EIGHTEEN

The whole Abbey plunged into mourning. There had been no thought of the Abbot dying for many years, so the stone carvers had not even begun working on the marble tomb that would take its place in the crypt with the other abbots and dignitaries. It didn't matter, though.

"I had to insist we first put Father Abbot in the ground," Brother Sebastien told me. "We will put him in the tomb when the Plague has been wasted away from his body."

While the worms did their work, Brother Joel began his, basing his carving on drawings of the Abbot Brother Marc provided for him. I imagined the Abbot, just bones, wearing his abbot robes and hat, the way the abbots and bishops looked in Brother Marc's death drawings. I didn't like thinking of the Abbot that way.

As we sang the Pie Jesu at his funeral Mass, I looked at all the empty stalls in the monk's chapel. I wondered how many more there would be.

Lord Morley attended the funeral. I saw him later, walking in the cloisters with the Prior, the two of them talking closely and earnestly.

The Prior took command of the abbey. In ordinary times, the Bishop would have made him abbot, but that would have to wait. The Bishop was still hiding from the Plague on his country estate. It didn't matter. The Prior was in charge.

The Prior enlisted the help of Lord Morley's men to send the crowd outside the abbey walls away for the three days of mourning. The day the mourning was over, the crowd came back.

It was not the prayerful, well-behaved pack of pilgrims that had taken Gaston from us. This was a needy crowd, insistent, and, as the day went on without an appearance from Micah, it became an angry crowd.

"Micah! Micah!" they yelled.

When the Company of Fools, with Micah and me in the donkey cart, finally moved through the gatehouse and out into the world, the crowd went wild.

"Save us, Micah! Save us!"

People reached up to touch him. They reached for me, too. We were both small boys. The crowd didn't know which was Micah.

"Get out of the cart!" Micah ordered me. "Some of them think you are me!"

"But I always ride with you as far as the Paris walls."

"Get out of the cart!" Micah gave me a shove that sent me tumbling. Brother Marc helped me down.

The Company went to the top of a small rise in the ground, so the crowd could see us. Brother Kenneth stepped forward, then had to step back again, to let the trumpeters blow their horns. Before they could say their piece, though, Brother Kenneth stepped in front of them.

"We are the Company of Fools," he boomed. "We are here to bring you the healing power of joy! So listen and laugh and be glad at all there is in the world that is good!"

We launched into our opening song. The crowd listened for a while, then began chanting again, "Micah! Micah!"

Micah stopped them. He rose up in the donkey cart and raised his hands for silence.

The crowd gave it to him.

When the crowd was silent, Micah began to sing, not the bishop song, but a ballad with a melody full of sad memories and hopes for a better day to come. His voice, after nearly a year of Brother Paul's careful training, was clearer than the finest bell, and sweeter than the loveliest bird. If anyone's voice could cure the Plague, Micah's could. It soared out over the crowd gathered on the green, and settled down on them, calming them, helping them to feel human again.

At the end of the song, the crowd remained quiet. Micah looked down at Brother Bart. "We can go now," he said. Brother Bart took the reins of the donkey, and we made our way into Paris.

Lord Morley's messengers had done their job well. People were waiting for us everywhere we went. They pressed in on us with their chants and their disease and their despair. Was Micah afraid? I don't know. I was. I stayed firmly sheltered between brothers Kenneth and Marc.

The city hadn't smelled as bad when the weather was cold. Now, with the approach of spring, stench was everywhere. The Plague was taking people faster and faster. Bodies were rotting on every street corner and in every gully. I began to believe that the Plague must be in the very air we were breathing. I fingered my Abracadabra charm through my tunic, and tried to take shallow breaths.

The trumpeters had something new to say this time. "The miraculous voice of this child of wonder has even more power to cure when the listener brings him a tribute!"

People in the crowd began to bring forth gifts—coins, jewelry, fine clothes, and household objects, rich and poor. They lifted them into the donkey cart, placing them at Micah's feet. I saw Micah's eyes grow wide as he ran his fingers through the coins. He could not count, of course, but I knew it was more than we'd made selling Abracadabras, and more than he'd ever seen at one time singing in the streets of Paris.

"We are not doing this for money!" Brother Bart exclaimed. He looked to me like he was having a hard time controlling his temper.

"Ask your prior," the trumpeter replied, then went back to calling to the crowd to give Micah their money.

"This is not why we began the Company of Fools," I heard Brother Jude say to the other monks. "We began it to minister to people's spirits, not take advantage of their desperation."

"If we take these gifts, we are no better than the scoundrels selling Plague spells and oils," Brother Marc said. "I think we should stop this now, go back to the abbey, and stay there."

"We are under Holy Obedience, Brother."

"To give obedience to something that is wrong is an even greater wrong."

My head swiveled from one brother to another. I wanted to turn around and go home, but I knew Micah wanted to keep singing. And, in a strange way, I was interested in what was happening. I knew that when the Pestilence ended, I would either be dead or confined again behind the abbey walls. I was not quite ready for either.

Micah was singing again, not bothering to wait

for his introduction. The monks continued their deliberations, but before they could reach a conclusion, we were all interrupted by the most terrible thing I had ever seen.

We heard them before we saw them. It began as a low rumbling, like distant thunder before a storm. It came closer and closer, until it presented itself in the square before us.

It was a group of men, stripped to the waist, with wild fringes of hair on all their faces. Their bodies and hair were smeared with manure. Even in this time of great stink, the stench that rose off them made me recoil. They recited chants of repentance, over and over, louder and louder, as they marched around in a circle. They thrashed their own backs with whips, the blows they gave themselves growing more powerful as their chants grew louder.

This was not the mild discipline the monks gave themselves from time to time (and which Micah and I had secretly witnessed from the catacombs). This was something fierce and crazy, like wild animals gone mad, although no animal I had ever known would do that kind of damage to itself.

Their screeches rent the air, and the whips tore their flesh until their faces and torsos ran with blood. Their teeth were bared like the fangs of monsters. They were moving closer and closer to us.

With such great suffering all around us, with so

many people in the world who wished in vain to be well, this spectacle of deliberate pain and disfiguration was too horrible to bear.

I began to scream. One of the brothers lifted me in his arms and buried my head in his shoulder, so I wouldn't have to look. "We're leaving right now!" he bellowed, and I knew then it was Brother Kenneth who carried me.

"They are the Flagellants," Brother Kenneth said into my ear as we walked. "They believe if they fast for weeks and do not wash, and if they make holes in their skin with whips and nails, they will not get the Plague. They are only men, Henri," he said. "That's all they are. Just foolish men with a bad idea."

By the time we reached the city gates, my fright had subsided into ordinary tears. Brother Kenneth lifted me into the donkey cart beside Micah. Micah, my old friend, took care of me.

He remained my old friend until we got back to the abbey, and the question of money came up.

"Of course the money is mine. People gave it to me," Micah stated. I remember so clearly how he squared his shoulders, curled his hands into stubborn fists, and glared up at Brother Bart.

"But we have taken a vow of poverty," Brother Bart said.

"You have. I haven't."

"It is wrong to make money from the suffering of others," Brother Bart tried.

"I didn't give them the Plague," Micah replied. "I simply sang them a song. That is my trade. I am a troubador. They were paying me for my service."

"You are a choirboy," Brother Bart said. "You owe your life to the Abbey of St. Luc."

"I owe my life to my good voice," Micah answered. "If I had been a bad singer, or no singer at all, would you have rescued me from the gallows that day? Still," he conceded, "you may be partly right. I'll share this payment with you. You can have the jewelry, the household goods, and the clothes.

I'll keep the money."

"That is not for you to decide," Brother Bart said. "That is the Prior's decision."

"I thought the Prior took a vow of poverty."

Brother Bart looked totally perplexed. He opened and closed his mouth several times, as if hoping some answer would come out of it, but none came. He threw up his hands and walked away. Micah grinned widely and jiggled the coins in his hands.

"You might have backed me up," he said, as we headed into the tunnels.

I couldn't see why the abbey should get all the money, either, but something about this didn't seem right. "St. Paul said the love of money is the root of all evil."

"I love money because I love to eat. The more money I have, the more I can eat. What's evil about that?"

"You don't pay for your food here."

"Sure I do," he said, "I pay for it with my singing. How long do you think they'd keep feeding me if I stopped singing?"

I thought about this as we entered the crypt, to our hiding place at the back. I tried one more time. "I think Brother Bart thinks it's bad for you to keep the money. Bad for your spirit," I said, as I watched Micah add the day's singing money to our Abracadabra earnings.

"It's only money," Micah said. "How can it be bad for my spirit?"

I didn't know. I wasn't doing any better than Brother Bart.

Money is mysterious to me, almost as mysterious as women. I don't understand what it does to people. I don't understand what it is to want to be rich, just like I don't understand what it is to be hungry. Can I understand those things without experiencing them? Can I ever gain wisdom if I don't understand them? The older I get, the less I seem to know.

I was afraid for Micah. I didn't know what I was afraid of, or how to tell him, or how to make him safe. I couldn't even name what the danger was.

My frustration made me angry. Micah and I began to quarrel over foolish, unrelated things. We avoided each other. I was not a very good friend, and it shames me now.

Brother Bart came up with what he thought was a solution for the next Company of Fools visit to Paris. "We will have no cart," he said. "Micah is a strong lad, he can walk to Paris with the rest of us."

When Lord Morley's men heard that, they went straight to the Prior. Their solution, and the one we had to live with, was to attach another cart behind the one Micah traveled in. People were directed to place their offerings there. Many did, especially the larger gifts. Some still dropped coins in Micah's cart.

Perhaps they believed that if they gave money directly to Micah, their chances of being spared the Plague were much greater. I don't know.

At the end of each trip, when we got back to the abbey, Micah gathered up his coins and hid them away. He no longer took me with him to the hiding place.

The Prior's officials and Lord Morley's messengers divided up the rest.

We saw the Flagellants again, many times. Along with their chants of "I am not worthy," they had new ones: "Kill the Jews! The Jews cause Plague! Kill the Jews!"

"Keep saying to yourself, 'They are only foolish men. They are only foolish men,'" Brother Bart suggested, to keep me from being scared. I tried that, and it helped, but not much. Just because men are foolish, it doesn't mean they are not dangerous.

How many different things had been blamed for causing the Plague! Pointed shoes, disobedient children, too much laughter, not enough laughter, the planets, an earthquake, ugly old women, lepers, Gypsies, not eating enough dates or filberts, breathing bad air, drinking bad water, saying the wrong prayers, drinking too much wine, not drinking enough wine, and now the Jews.

Everyone had a scapegoat. No one had the truth. Maybe those who come after us will find out the truth, will come to know truly how all those people died. I am not hopeful. From what I have seen, people get stupider as they get older. As it is with men, so it must be for the human race.

Micah's voice seemed to take on a new power just then. It was always special, but now it seemed to have a calming effect on a crowd. They would approach the Company of Fools, their faces twisted with grief and pain and fear. Micah would sing, and I watched the anguish drain from their faces. They went away calmer, feeling, I think, a little better. Not even greedy Lord Morley with his grasping trumpeters could take that away from what was happening.

I don't know if Micah's voice kept anyone from getting the Plague, or cured anyone who already had it. We went to a different part of Paris on every trip, even entering the city by different gates. We never saw Micah's failures.

We heard plenty about his successes, though. Each time the trumpeters spoke, the numbers of people he saved grew. The more they said he saved, the more offerings people gave. I don't know if the trumpeters believed what they told the crowds. I only know what they kept saying.

And I know that Micah believed it.

"Micah," I said one day, just as we returned from the city, "if you can really stop this Plague, don't you think you had better go ahead and do it?"

Micah turned to me, his face a strange mixture

of fear and defiance. "I'll stop it when I'm good and ready," he said. "Actually, I think I'll let it go on for a good long while. It's making me rich."

Then I did something I never, ever imagined I would do.

I punched Micah right in the nose.

I'll never understand why he didn't punch me back.

I don't remember exactly when this happened, but I'm going to write it into my chronicle now, because I am remembering it now. One night, Rafe woke up crying. I heard Micah stir in the cot next to me. I opened my eyes and watched him get out of bed and go to Rafe's side. I saw him hug the small boy, and rub his back until his sobs were quiet. He wiped the tears from Rafe's face with his hands.

Micah picked up Felix, the schoolhouse dog, from the foot of Oswin's bed where he usually slept, and tucked him in with Rafe. Then he sang quiet, happy little songs until Rafe fell back asleep. He sat on the edge of Rafe's bed for a long, long time, watching him sleep.

Bad dreams and cries in the night became regular in the choirboys' dormitory. We laughed about them in the morning, and teased unmercifully the one who had cried out during the night. Each one of us— even Arlo, even Micah—called out in the darkness from time to time. There was no shame in it. Death was all around us, and everyone thought the world was coming to a painful, bloody end.

When fear woke me up, I reached under my bed for my astrolabe, and hugged it close to me. I imagined my father coming to be with me, his face thick with whiskers, and the smell of the sea upon him. I have never smelled the sea, but when I do, I will recognize it at once.

As I write this, I realize I am contradicting myself. I have written repeatedly that my life will be lived within the comforting confines of these walls, that it will be dedicated to reading and writing and searching out original thought. Usually, those are my plans. What I have seen of this world and its people has made me want to live apart from them.

At other times, I yearn to go to the great university in Paris, where Arlo will soon go. I can learn much from the books in the abbey. But, although many of the monks are learned men, the abbey is not a place for extended discussion and argument. Arlo says university is all about arguing. I think I would like that. I think that would make my mind grow.

I have mentioned, too, how I want to go to the ocean with my father's astrolabe. Still another thought has come to me since I began to write this chronicle. Maybe I could become a chronicler for real, and travel with popes and kings, writing down their battles and exploits for the benefit of history.

I like the idea of my words being the ones that give shape to the past for the generations that come after us.

Monk, scholar, chronicler—you will have to live with the contradictions in this chronicle. You have no choice. I am writing it, and the person who controls the pen controls the ideas. I may be small and insignificant in myself, but my words have authority. They will settle into your mind, and you will think of me and my tale while you go about the other duties of your life. I am just a choirboy, and when you find and read this, I am probably long dead. But my words live on. *That* is power.

And now I will go back to my tale.

"There are going to be changes," the Prior said.

The Company of Fools was assembled in his study. It used to be Father Abbot's study. It had been a warm place, then. I looked around. Nothing had been changed or moved, but everything was different.

"First off, you will no longer wear those ridiculous costumes. I see no virtue in monks looking like fools. Second, you will no longer sing songs that poke fun at the Church. I see no virtue in that, either."

Brother Bart spoke for all of us. "Father Prior, the whole idea of the Company of Fools is to make people laugh, to give them some moments of joy and comfort in this time of horror."

"Joy and comfort on this earth are of no consequence," the Prior stated flatly.

"Memento mori," I mumbled.

"Exactly."

"Then there is no purpose for our being together," Brother Bart said.

"There is," the Prior said. "You will be escorts for Micah. All of you. Micah is very valuable to us. He must be accompanied and protected when he goes out into the world."

"I must protest," Brother Bart began.

"I hear your protest. Now, you must do as you are told. Micah, you will no longer wear the bishop's miter. Such mockery is unseemly. We have something new for you to wear." The Prior rang a bell on his desk. An assistant brought in a new tunic and cape. Micah's eyes lit up as the prior held the garments up for him to see.

The tunic was white with trimmings of gold thread. The cape flowed like an angel's robe. Everything shimmered and glowed, and Micah beamed with pride. The Prior smiled at Micah, and Micah smiled back at the Prior, and suddenly I didn't know my own friend.

We went back out into the world. We were no longer a Company of Fools. We were now the Company of Micah.

The brothers wore their regular black robes, with the addition of a white sash across their chest. I had to wear a pageboy's uniform, borrowed from Lord

Morley. My job was supposed to be serving Micah, but I didn't do it. I would go with him because he was my friend. I would sing with the monks, giving background to Micah's voice, because the monks were my friends. But no one could make me be Micah's servant.

"You have to wait on me," Micah insisted. "You heard the Prior. I'm valuable. I am the abbey's wonder child."

"The Prior never got anything right in his life," I replied. "And you're just a boy from the gutter."

This did not help our friendship.

Lord Morley sent armed men to guard Micah, and to guard the offerings people made. Micah no longer sat in a donkey cart. He rode in a high wagon that was draped in scarlet and pulled by two fine, white abbey horses. When he wasn't singing, he sat on a large, high-backed chair that made him seem even smaller than he really was. The offerings got piled up behind him.

The brothers were supposed to collect the gifts that people brought, but I never saw any of them do that. Lord Morley's people did the collecting, with eagerness. For every item that went into the wagon, an item disappeared into the pockets and pouches of Lord Morley's men. Lots of people were getting rich.

"What's that?" I asked Micah one night, as we were getting ready for bed in the dormitory.

"I was wondering how long it would take you to notice," he said, dangling the gold medallion in front of my face. "Father Prior thought I should have this."

"What for?"

"For being me, of course."

"But the Pickle doesn't like you."

"He likes me well enough to give me a medallion."

"Micah, are you bragging again?" Arlo asked, from the other end of the dormitory. "I suppose you think we should wash your feet for you."

"Somebody should wash his feet!" Fabien said.

"I think we should dump him down the necessarium again," Oswin suggested.

"His head is too big now. He'd never fit through the hole," said Bayard.

"You're all just envious!" Micah said, slamming himself into bed. "Envy is a sin, you know."

"So is pride," Arlo said. "So is greed. So is bearing false witness."

Micah didn't answer our head boy. He stared up at the ceiling, rubbing his medallion, until the candles were blown out.

"Micah?" I whispered.

"What is it?" he whispered back.

"Who are you?"

He didn't answer me, either.

And then, the unthinkable happened. One of the choirboys came down with the Plague.

It was Rafe, the smallest of us.

Arlo was the one who noticed it, trying to rouse him in the morning.

"Hurry up, Rafe, get out of bed," Arlo called. "If you let the others get to the breakfast table ahead of you, there won't be anything left to eat by the time you get there. You know what hogs they are."

Agreeably, most of us made pig noises as we pulled our tunics on. Arlo went over to Rafe's cot to shake him awake, then backed away in horror.

"Rafe has Plague!" he exclaimed. Then, remembering he was head boy, and beyond panic, he began to give orders. "Bayard, run and get Brother Sebastien." Bayard was our fastest runner. "The rest of you, outside on the green. Take the porridge and bowls with you and eat breakfast on the grass."

I grabbed Rafe's friend Reverdy, who was already weeping, and ran.

We were down the dormitory stairs and out of the schoolhouse before Arlo finished his instructions. We ran out, leaving poor Rafe to battle the Plague without us. Even Arlo came out, after covering Rafe up with the blanket from his own cot.

"Did anyone bring breakfast out?" Arlo asked when he joined us outside the schoolhouse. No one had. No one was hungry. "Did Bayard go for Brother

Sebastien?" Bayard had. "So we'll all just sit out here and wait, then."

"How did it get in there?" Hugh asked. "And why Rafe? Everyone likes Rafe."

"Why did the Abbot die instead of the Prior?" Arlo asked, as an answer. "Shut up with your foolish questions."

"Hey! Where's Micah?" I looked around the group of us. At the same moment, I heard a now familiar sound.

"Is that idiot in there singing?" Oswin asked.

"He's not an idiot," I said.

"He's an idiot if he thinks he can cure Rafe by singing to him."

"He's only trying to make Rafe feel better," I said.

Arlo gave us all a long look, then he did what I should have been the first to have done. He turned and went back inside the dormitory.

"What does he think he's doing?" Oswin asked.

"He's going to pull that idiot out of there," said Joris.

"No, he's not," I said, but I don't know how I knew that.

I was right. In a moment, Arlo's rich alto voice joined Micah's sweet soprano as they sang Dona Nobis Pacem.

I should be inside with them, I told myself. For Rafe, and for Micah. But I didn't move.

Hugh went in then, joined soon by Fabien,

Antoine, and Oswin. By the time Bayard returned with Brother Sebastien, most of the choir was standing by Rafe's bed, singing to him. Only the weeping Reverdy remained outside. And me.

Brother Bart came out of nowhere. He put his arm around my shoulder.

"Micah thinks he can cure Rafe. But he can't, can he?" I said.

Brother Sebastien carried little Rafe out of the schoolhouse in his arms, and ran with him toward the infirmary. Micah ran after them, still singing. The boys gathered in the schoolhouse doorway and watched silently as Brother Bart grabbed onto Micah as Micah ran by. Micah punched and kicked at Brother Bart, but Brother Bart held fast until Brother Sebastien had time to get Rafe into the infirmary and secure the door.

"If Rafe dies, it will be your fault!" Micah screamed at Brother Bart, giving him a final shove and breaking away. We watched him run toward the infirmary.

"He didn't mean it." I said.

"He did," Brother Bart replied, sadly. "I just hope that someday, he won't."

Rafe died three days later. Brother Sebastien's attentions didn't help. Micah's singing didn't help. The monks' prayers didn't help. Nothing helped.

CHAPTER TWENTY-ONE

One foot in front of the other. Follow the lines. Around and around, no beginning and no end.

I was walking the labyrinth, by myself, late at night while the abbey was asleep.

I just couldn't stay in the dormitory. Every time I closed my eyes, I saw Rafe. Every time I tried to sleep, I pictured a grinning skeleton coming for all of us choirboys, like in one of Brother Marc's drawings. I couldn't stay in bed.

Around and around the pattern on the floor of the nave I walked. I kept my eyes on my feet, and didn't think of anything.

I heard the sound of another's footsteps on the stone floor. I didn't turn around. I didn't need to. I knew it was Micah.

We didn't speak. We didn't sing. We just walked.

Each morning began with a roll call. We were afraid that the Plague might have developed a taste for choirboys and was planning to devour us all. Each sunrise, though, saw all our heads rise from the pillows.

"Is anyone dead yet?"

"I'm dead," someone would say, and someone else would rise from his bed, clutching his throat, making choking noises and collapse on the floor. One day, we decided to all be dead. We rubbed ash into our faces. We sat at the refectory table, with our hoods pulled up, chanting the Latin death verbs: *mortuus sum, mortuus es, mortuus est, mortui sumus, mortui estis, mortui sunt.* We thought we were terribly funny.

Micah joined us in these things. It almost felt like old times.

That ended as soon as he got into his new white tunic and climbed into his scarlet wagon. Then he became the abbey's wonder child, and was far away from me.

We went on this way for a while. The people we saw in the streets didn't look so scared anymore. They just looked tired. That was how I was beginning to feel. Very, very tired.

Micah was too.

"I don't want to do it anymore."

"What did you say?"

"Father Prior, I don't want to do it anymore."

If Micah knew I was listening at the secret door behind the study, he gave no sign of it.

There was an icy silence. I could just imagine the Pickle's face.

"People aren't responding to my voice like they used to. I used to be able to make them feel better. Now, it doesn't seem to matter to them if I sing or not. Everyone seems so tired."

Still, the Prior said nothing.

"Besides," Micah continued, "it hasn't been the same since Rafe died. If my voice really can cure the Plague, why didn't it cure Rafe? No, Brother Bart was right. I don't have special powers. I'm just a boy."

Now the Prior spoke. His voice was quiet, which made it seem meaner, somehow.

"Brother Bart has never been right about anything, ever," he said. "You will continue singing, just as you have been doing."

"But I've just told you I want to stop. You and Lord Morley must have enough offerings by now."

Bang! The Prior slammed something on the desk, making a big noise, and making me jump. "Those gifts are for God, not for myself!"

Micah laughed at that. "I'm not one of your monks, Father Prior. I don't have to believe you. And I don't have to obey you."

Out in the passageway, I wanted to dance. Micah was back!

But the Prior hadn't finished. I heard him rise from his chair.

"I don't intend to explain the workings of the Church to a gutter urchin like you. You will obey me, or you will wish Brother Bart had left you to hang."

"You can't do anything to me! I've survived much worse than you. I'll leave you now to play with your gold—excuse me, God's gold. I have to go apologize to my friends. I've been behaving like an ass. I've been behaving like you."

"You'll do as I say or you will die."

That stopped Micah. "You can't do that. Thou shalt not kill, remember? You're supposed to believe in that."

"When the enemies of the Church show their ugly faces, regrettably, blood must be shed to cleanse the atmosphere of evil."

"Sounds like one of your stupid speeches from the marketplace."

"You are an ignorant boy, so I shall rise above your impertinence, but hear this. You will do as I say, or I will bring you up on charges of heresy, blasphemy, and black magic. I will summon the Holy Inquisition, and you will be put on trial for casting a spell over people, making them believe you could cure the Plague."

"No one will believe that!"

"Abracadabra," the Prior said. "People will

believe what they are told to believe."

Micah's voice trembled. I knew it was from rage, not from fear. "You are an evil man. But you'll have to find me first. I'll leave this abbey right now and disappear into the streets of Paris. You'll never put me before your stupid Inquisition."

"Go then. It doesn't matter. The Church will be content with the trials of your accomplices—Brother Marc and Brother Kenneth, Brother Joel and Brother Bart, of course. And your little friend, Henri."

"Henri!"

"Evil comes in all shapes and sizes," the Prior said calmly.

My heart was beating so hard I was afraid it would be heard inside the study.

"By the time the Court of Inquisition gets through with your friends, they will welcome the flames. You do know the Inquisition burns people at the stake, don't you? After torture, of course—they must be given the opportunity to confess. Confession is so good for the soul."

"But they're not true, those things you said."

"Truth can be a very flexible commodity," the Prior said.

Micah sighed, defeated. "All right. You win. What do you want me to do?"

"Just as you have been doing. Nothing could be simpler. And I think you had better stay here with me from now on. Such an important child as you shouldn't sleep in a drafty dormitory with common choirboys." He rang the bell on his desk. One of Lord Morley's armed men came in. I could hear the clank of his sword. "Find a nice room for Micah," he directed the guard, "one where he will not be troubled by the outside world."

From the sounds of fighting, I gathered Micah was trying to give the guard a bloody nose. Micah was a good fighter, but the guard was much bigger.

The guard took Micah away, and I tiptoed out of the passage, along the catacombs, to find the others. We met, as usual, in the wine cellar.

"The Holy Inquisition." Brother Bart said the words slowly. "We shall have to be careful. We shall have to be very, very careful."

Brother Bart came up with the plan. We all talked about it, at secret meetings in the wine cellar attended by the choirboys and the Company of Fools. Everyone played a part. The biggest job was left for me to carry out.

The Prior helped, in a way. He kept Micah locked up in his house for nearly two weeks. That gave us time to plan.

"How do we know Micah's all right?" Oswin wondered.

"Micah is valuable to the Prior," Arlo said, "and to Lord Morley. They're not going to hurt him."

"We will have to trust that Micah can take care of himself," Brother Kenneth said. "We cannot arouse suspicion by trying to see him."

The Prior helped us there, too. He and Lord Morley decided to hold a grand procession into Paris, on the day the Lendit Fair would have opened. There was no fair this year, because of the Pestilence, and the procession could be all about

Chapter Twenty-Two

Micah. The choir would sing behind Micah on the platform.

Although he was taken away again right after rehearsals, at least we got to see him. We made faces at him, and he made faces back, so we knew he was all right.

On the day of the procession, Micah rode in the scarlet wagon. He looked sad and lonely. I tried to catch his eye, to give him a smile and wave, but he wasn't looking at any of us choirboys.

I felt sorry for him. I knew what was in store for him today. Things would get worse before they got better.

The Prior may have hoped for a procession as glorious as the last one to the Lendit Fair, but times had changed. Many monks had died. Other abbeys, in the grip of the Plague, did not send monks to join us. There were no new banners. Father Prior's grand procession wasn't grand all.

Lord Morley and his men were with us. Two of his horses were pulling an empty wagon. It looked to me as though Lord Morley and the Prior were expecting a lot of contributions.

We proceeded to the same square we opened the fair from last year. We mounted the same platform, but it was a different world we looked out on. There were no entertainers or amusements. The people in the square were not celebrating. No one looked pleased to see our procession.

We sang the opening hymn. The Prior spoke the words of the blessing, and Lord Morley spoke about the miracle of Micah saving his daughter. Then Lord Morley's men gave their usual exhortations to the crowd.

"Come forward with your tributes for young Micah, wonder child of St. Luc's! Bring him your gifts, that his voice might save you from the Plague."

I looked over at Brother Bart. He nodded. Now was the time.

I stepped out of the line of choirboys. The others filled in the space so I wouldn't be missed. Just as Micah began to sing, I climbed down from the platform, shielded by the Company of Fools, and slipped into the crowd.

I went to work.

"Young Micah is a fake," I said to the first person I came to. "He can't cure the Plague. They're lying to you to get your money. Young Micah is a fake."

I darted through the crowd, saying my message over and over. I said things to make the crowd turn on my friend.

It was easy. People were tired. They had lost so much and been afraid for so long. They were tired of suffering, and they were tired of hoping.

The crowd was in the mood to disbelieve. All I did was say out loud something they had been thinking anyway. No one in Paris believed Micah was special that day, except for a handful of choir-boys and monks. He was special because he was our friend. For us, he didn't need any magical power beyond that.

"Young Micah is a fake!" I kept saying.

"You're right," a man said. "He is a fake! My wife and daughter heard him sing. I gave him all my money to cure them. They still died of the Plague!"

"Fake!" someone nearby screamed out.

The crowd needed no more prompting than that. "Fake! You're a fake!" Others joined in the cry.

People began to throw things at Micah. Soon the whole crowd was cursing him and throwing mud and rocks at him. I was surprised at how little effort it took to make a whole crowd of people hate someone.

People were throwing things without aiming. Some of the mud hit Lord Morley's men. A big blob hit the Prior right in the face. Another hit Micah in the chest. He stood and stared at the splotch of filth on his shiny white tunic.

His worshipers had turned on him.

Everything seemed to move very slowly, but I know that the monks moved with great speed to get the choirboys out of sight of the crowd. Brother Kenneth, his arms strong from lifting wine barrels, snatched Micah from the platform. The monks opened ranks to let them pass, then closed up again, to hide the view.

Lord Morley and his men vanished as soon as the crowd turned against them. The armed guards went with them. There was no one to keep the crowd away. The people began to move toward the platform. Being small is an advantage at times like these. I darted through the crowd and joined up with my friends. The monks had surrounded the choirboys and were helping them onto the wagons.

The Prior did not help himself much. He cursed the crowd. "You will all die!" he screamed. "You will all burn in hell for attacking the Church!" He did not frighten anyone. He only made people angrier. Someone threw a rock. It hit the Prior in the head and he dropped to the ground.

"The Prior's down," I said, cheerfully.

"We must rescue him," Brother Bart said.

"Why?" I asked. He didn't answer me. He was already at the Prior's side. I joined him there. The two of us dragged the Prior off the platform. Brother Kenneth helped us get him into the wagon.

"Why did we do that?" I asked. "He's an awful man."

"He's also a human being," Brother Bart said. "And more importantly, so are we."

We loaded the wagons with choirboys and monks, and headed out of Paris as fast as the crowd would let us. They kept throwing things and screaming, but eventually, we left them behind.

The Prior lay at our feet. He was alive, but the rock had knocked him out. He looked insignificant, lying there on the floor of the wagon.

"He'll have an awful headache when he wakes up," Arlo said.

"A headache for a headache," Oswin said.

It was a pretty feeble joke, but we laughed and laughed. Micah laughed the loudest of all. When his laughter turned to sobbing, Brother Bart held him and let him cry.

The hit on the head kept the Prior in his bed for a week. None of us were sorry.

The joyful catastrophe of the procession put us all in an extremely good mood. We had much to celebrate. There was still a bit of summer left, the season of fun. We'd never have to be the Company of Micah again. And Micah was back to being my friend. I had everything I needed.

The Plague seemed to be co-operating, too. There were fewer deaths among the brothers. There were no new Plague victims, and Brother Sebastien sent the survivors back into the community.

Brother Sebastien had time to spend with me again. We gathered and dried herbs, and talked of medicine and science. We did not speak of the Plague. There were too many other things to talk about.

Brother Bart and Micah went back to walking along the inside of the abbey walls. I saw them together often. They were always talking.

One night, late in September, we had visitors in

the schoolhouse. Monks from the Company of Fools came in, each one bearing food and drink for a feast. We ate and drank and laughed far into the night.

Late in the evening, I noticed that Micah had fallen silent. "What's wrong?" I asked him.

"It's not finished," he said.

"What do you mean?"

"I think we should go out again."

Everyone was listening. "You mean the Company of Fools?" Brother Marc asked. He was smiling.

"One last time," Micah said. "Just for us. Just to finish it off right."

"What do you mean finish it?" I asked, but my question was lost in the excitement Micah's suggestion created.

"Can we all go?" Oswin asked. "We can act like fools."

"You, most particularly," Arlo said, but Oswin just laughed.

"I suppose we should ask the Prior's permission," Brother Jude said.

No one offered to do that. I was not surprised.

By the time we had fetched the costumes from a trunk in the storage room, it was time for the brothers to go to the cathedral for the night prayers. We went up to bed.

"Micah," I whispered, after the candles had been put out. "What did you mean, finish it off?"

Micah didn't answer for a while. Then he said, "I have to make it right. That's all. I just have to make things right." I heard him roll over in his cot, and knew he would say no more that night.

We headed out the next morning. Brother Marc had managed to find costume items for each choir-boy from among things people had left behind at the guesthouse.

"Where's my court jester costume?" I asked, rummaging through the pile of clothing.

I heard Micah say, "Your costume is on the chair," and looked. All that was there was the Boy Bishop's robe and miter.

"Your turn to be the bishop," Micah said. I looked at him. *He* was dressed as the court jester.

We went out into the world again for a day. We performed in villages and along the road, wherever there were people who looked like they could use cheering up.

I sang the Boy Bishop's songs. I didn't sing them as well as Micah—I don't have his sort of voice. But I did all right. People laughed at us, and we laughed with them, and everyone felt better.

Everywhere we went, I saw Micah dip his hand into a bag he carried, bring out some coins, and give them to the poor people we came across. I under-stood. He was giving away his Plague money. He was making things right.

Micah and I spent the whole next day together. We did all of our favorite things. We went swimming and fishing, we eavesdropped on the monks, we ate apples off the trees, played with the young pigs, and chased the chickens around the yard. We played a wonderful game of Ghost Jump with the other boys. At the end of the day, Micah and I went up to the top of the bell tower, and watched for shooting stars.

"Things are going to be easier from now on," I said. "It's been a very bad year, but things are going to be better from now on."

"The Prior is still around," Micah said.

"Who cares about him? We've dealt with him before. Remember the way his face looked when he drank that bitter wine? We can handle the Prior. Don't you worry about that."

"This is your home," Micah said.

"Of course. And it's your home, too."

"It's not my home," Micah said.

I got a cold feeling in my stomach. "What do you mean it's not your home?"

Micah turned away from me to look at the night sky. "Do you remember when we all came up here at the end of St. Nicholas Day last year?"

"That's the first time you were the Boy Bishop," I said. "We played all day, and came up here with all the choirboys. We yelled out at the world, and it began to snow."

"That was a good night," Micah said. "Let's do that again some day."

He wouldn't say anything more. We went back to the dormitory and went to bed. When I woke up the next morning, he was gone.

He left me his lute. That's the only goodbye he gave me.

For the next four weeks, I didn't say a word. I didn't sing in the cathedral. I didn't answer when the monks asked me a question. I didn't talk to the boys in the dormitory. If one of the brothers set me in front of some work, such as candlesticks to polish or dried herbs to grind, I would do it. But I did not seek out any labor.

I was furious with Micah. I felt abandoned and betrayed, and I was not prepared to be lonely again.

I did not know what to do with myself.

I walked, around and around the inside of the abbey walls, just like Brother Bart. The boys took to calling me Little Bart. They didn't tease me, though—Arlo wouldn't let them. But I don't think they wanted to, anyway.

No one knew what I was doing. No one knew that I was trying to decide which side of the wall I wanted to be on.

No one, except Brother Bart.

He joined me quite often. For weeks, we walked

in silence. Then one day he spoke.

"He didn't leave because he was afraid of the Prior," Brother Bart said. "He didn't leave because he no longer wanted to be your friend. And he didn't leave because he hated it here. Actually, he liked living here, very much."

"He left because he didn't know who he was anymore. He was no longer a street urchin. He was not a miracle worker. And, although he sang so beautifully, he was never truly a choirboy. What did that leave him? He had to find out, and he couldn't do that inside these walls."

"He could have asked me to go with him," I said.

"What would you have done if he'd asked you?"

I didn't know. Would I have dropped my studies, left the security of the abbey? "I would have gone," I said. "To be with Micah, I would have gone."

But even as I spoke the words, I doubted they were true. What I longed for was simply more of what I had already: the order and calm of the abbey, the hauntingly beautiful plainsong in the cathedral, the quiet thrill of understanding a new passage of Virgil.

"There is a time for everything," Brother Bart said. "When it is time for you to be out in the world again, you will know it."

"And what about Micah?"

"Don't you worry about Micah. You'll see him again."

I went back to singing in the cathedral and joking with the boys in the dormitory. They didn't ask me any questions. It was as if I had been away with one of my fevers.

Many weeks have passed since that morning Micah left. The Plague has left Paris, and abbey life has returned to the way it has been for hundreds of years, and will be for hundreds of years to come, should we be blessed with so much time. The abbey of St. Luc continues, even without Father Abbot, even without Micah.

The Plague took many of our monks, many that I didn't know, and some that I did. Brother Kenneth's great, booming voice was silenced forever in the final weeks of the Pestilence. Brother Stephen has taken over his chores in the wine cellar, and Brother Keith is now the baker as well as the gardener.

Brother Pascal the sacristan died, and Brother Beltran the Latin master, and Brother Nestor the cobbler, and Brother Kerrian the beekeeper.

Father Prior is dead, too. He did not die of Plague. Father Prior was entertaining Lord Morley in his private quarters. He ordered a chicken be slaughtered for their dinner. "Serve us the chicken that Brother Bart brought into the abbey," he ordered.

Brother Bart's chicken, the best egg-layer in the henhouse, was prepared as instructed. The Prior and Lord Morley settled down for a delicious meal.

Halfway through, the Prior choked on a chicken bone and died at his table.

If you suspect that this news was greeted with laughter and applause in the schoolhouse, and jokes about "choking on his own words," and outrageous mimicking of a pompous person gagging with his hands around his throat, you will find no clues here to confirm your suspicions, or deny them.

The monks held a conclave, and voted our steady, good housemaster, Brother Thomas, to be abbot-elect. His confirmation will have to wait until the Pope appoints a new bishop. Our old bishop was surprised by the Plague on his country estate, and died there. He ran from suffering, but it found him, in the end.

And yet Brother Sebastien, who spent every day of the Pestilence staring it down and comforting the afflicted, is still with us. Some of the monks who helped him have died. Others still chant the five services in Chapel every day and are very much alive. We still have Brother Marc, Brother Joel, and Brother Joseph. Brother Peter in the almshouse still cares for the poor who come to him.

Reverdy died, soon after Rafe, as did Garwood and Antoine. The rest of us choirboys are still here. If any boy's family is still alive, they'll soon come looking for their sons.

We are fortunate. We have heard from passing Franciscans of whole abbeys taken. There is one abbey where all but one died of the Plague. The one that is left must be terribly lonely.

We are also lucky in this abbey because there is food enough to see us through the winter, with some to spare for the almshouse. Travelers tell of bare fields, not planted in the spring or harvested in the autumn because the Plague took away the people who do those jobs. Whole flocks of sheep lay in pastures, dead of Plague, and cattle, untended, strayed from their homes. There will be many empty bellies this winter.

The Plague is gone, though. I know it is gone for good because of two things.

The first is that Brother Bart's rosebush lost its roses. They withered and dropped off the moment Brother Leo, the last monk to get the Plague, passed away. All the blossoms in the infirmary dried up, too, as if they knew they weren't needed anymore.

As Brother Sebastien said, life is a fine balance between magic and reason. Things we can't understand today we may be able to understand tomorrow, but there are also things that don't make logical sense, and for now, we just have to accept them. The challenge is in knowing what to accept as magic, and what to overcome as ignorance.

The second thing that assures me the Pestilence is gone is that Brother Bart's cat came back.

As soon as Brother Leo's body was taken away to

its place of final rest, Medicina hopped through the window, hissed at everyone, and looked around for someone's feet to warm.

I knew then that the world was not going to end. It will go on. Noah had his rainbow. St. Luc's has its cat.

I feel certain, too, as I write, that the world has learned a great lesson from the Plague. Having seen so much suffering, we will never again cause others to suffer. We will not let people go hungry when there is food to be had. We will not let people be cold when we have means to build shelter. We will talk to each other, and learn from each other, and never again will we kill each other in wars. We have seen enough death.

I, who have been lucky enough to survive the Plague when so many others did not, will go on, too. I will learn, and grow, and laugh when I can, and dance, like Micah, on the tops of tables.

It is cold in the scriptorium, and dark. This chronicle is now done, ready to be bound and hidden away in the crypt, for some future choirboy to find.

This is the night of the feast of St. Nicholas. When I finish this, I will go up to the top of the bell tower. I will look out at the great, glorious world, and wish Micah well, wherever he is.

Dum Vivimus, Vivamus
Henri of St. Luc's
Anno Domini 1349

HISTORICAL NOTE

The Plague, or Black Death as it later came to be known, swept through Asia and Europe at a time when scientific knowledge was outranked by superstition. Many people thought the world was coming to an end.

The swiftness of the disease contributed to its horror. The bubonic form, with its painful boils and dark blotches on the skin, was the slower killer, often making its victims suffer in terrible agony for days before killing them. The pneumonic form, which affected the lungs, killed in a day. There are many recorded tales of people going to bed at night, seemingly healthy, and being dead of the Plague by morning.

Although physicians of the time didn't know it, the cause of the Plague was the common black rat, with the Latin name *rattus rattus*. The infected rats came to Europe in merchant ships from Asia. Fleas bit the rats, then bit humans, and thus the Plague was spread.

People dealt with the horror of the Plague in different ways. Many wealthy people retreated to country estates where they ate well and were lavishly entertained, believing they could hide from the Plague this way. Others found people to blame, and there were many massacres of Jews and old women, on the foolish assumption that they were the cause. Some people took to drinking and carousing, others to prayer and fasting. It didn't matter what they did. The Plague took them anyway.

Roughly twenty-five million people, a third of Europe's population, were killed by the Plague by the time it fizzled out, in 1350. When it returned again a decade later, it killed another 10 million. It was to keep returning, with varying force, over the next few hundred years.

The Plague shook people's belief in the power and divine right of both the clergy and the nobility. These doubts paved the way for land and labor reform, and for the Renaissance, with its new ideas about science, art and society.

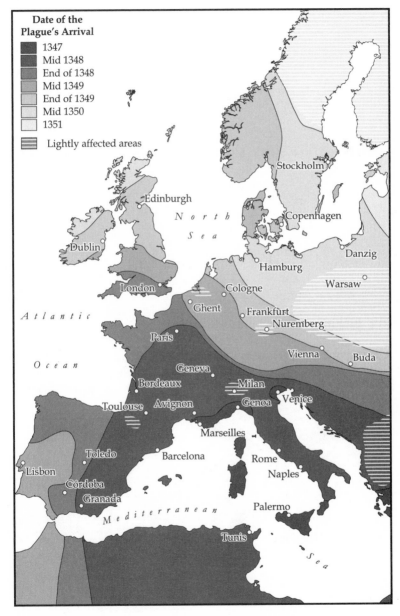

Date of the Plague's Arrival
- 1347
- Mid 1348
- End of 1348
- Mid 1349
- End of 1349
- Mid 1350
- 1351
- Lightly affected areas

Stockholm

N o r t h S e a

Edinburgh

Copenhagen

Dublin

Danzig

Hamburg

Warsaw

London

Cologne

Ghent

Frankfurt

A t l a n t i c

Paris

Nuremberg

O c e a n

Vienna

Buda

Geneva

Bordeaux

Milan

Venice

Toulouse

Avignon

Genoa

Marseilles

Toledo

Barcelona

Rome

Naples

Lisbon

Córdoba

Granada

Palermo

M e d i t e r r a n e a n

Tunis

S e a

GLOSSARY

abbey: (male) religious community and its living place

abbot: the head of a (male) religious community

altar: table in a church where Eucharist rituals take place

astrolabe: medieval instrument for navigation

bishop: high-ranking church officer

bishop's miter: an arch-shaped hat

catacombs: system of underground tombs

cathedral: the most important church of a given area containing the bishop's throne

censer: incense burner

cesspit: hole in the ground over which an outhouse is built

chancel: area of a cathedral in front of and around the altar

chapter house: meeting in which the running of an abbey is discussed; place where this meeting is held

cloisters: covered walkways

compline: night prayer service

crucifer: person in a procession who carries a cross

Dies Irae: Latin, "day of anger"; part of a requiem

Eucharist: church service that commemorates the final meal Jesus Christ shared with his followers

habit: simple robe worn by monks and nuns

Holy Obedience: one of the vows a monk takes on entering an order

hornbook: tablet of wood and animal horn showing the alphabet and other simple text; used to teach reading

illuminator: illustrator of manuscripts

In Paradisum: Latin, "in Paradise"; part of a requiem

Inquisition: the court of the medieval Roman Catholic church

introit: music sung as part of the Eucharist

Kyrie, Kyrie Eleison: Greek, "have mercy on us"

last rites: ritual of confession and forgiveness for a person about to die

Mass: celebration of the Eucharist in the Roman Catholic church; the music that accompanies this service

matins: early morning prayer service

mortuus sum, mortuus es, mortuus est, mortui sumus, mortui estis, mortui sunt: Latin, "I am dead, you are dead, he is dead, we are dead, you are dead, they are dead"

Mother Superior: the head of a female religious community

nave: long central portion of a cathedral

necessarium: "necessary" room (outhouse)

parchment: animal skin prepared for writing on

Pie Jesu: Latin, "blessed Jesus"

plainsong: simple, rhythmless music sung in unison

prior: officer in an abbey second to the abbot

relic: ancient religious object

reliquary: container for a relic

requiem: church service for the dead

requiescat in pace: Latin, "may he rest in peace"

sacristan: person in charge of the equipment used in church services; equipment kept in a **sacristy**

Te Deum: Latin, "thee, O God"

vespers: evening prayer service

vestments: clothing used in church services; kept in a **vestry**